THE STEWARDESS'S DIARY - PART FIVE

IRELAND

S.M. PRATT

The Stewardess's Diary - Part Five: Ireland
Copyright © 2016 by S.M. Pratt

Last updated January 25th, 2020
Editing by Samantha Marie

ISBN: 978-0-9940630-8-3 (e-book)

ISBN: 978-1-988639-24-6 (paperback)

PROLOGUE

I'M CHARLIE, a veteran pilot for a major international airline that shall remain nameless for reasons you'll soon come to understand.

A year ago, while waiting for my flight to London in the airline's lounge at one of America's largest hubs, I discovered a special and highly personal journal among my belongings. How it happened, I'll never know, but the beautiful brown leather notebook nonetheless appeared in my briefcase at some point between the time I left my New York penthouse apartment and arrived at the airport lounge.

Perhaps it was a mix-up at security, or some devious stewardess with sly hand skills, but I've since become obsessed with the person who wrote that diary, her stories, and—to be blunt—her unconventional sex life.

My best friend—let's call him Bob—is one of my regular co-pilots. Bob advised me to forget about the journal and ignore my hunch to track down its rightful owner. After my initial reading of her hand-written accounts, the part of me who's loyal to the airline and wants the best for our passengers certainly needed to find that stewardess and expel her from our company—or whatever airline she's with. This woman is surely a threat to any crew with her irreverent disregard for our uniforms, her sexual behavior with passengers and airline employees, and the way she ignores regulations. She should clearly be punished for her conduct...

But after reading and re-reading each one of her journal entries, another, more animal part of me has grown fond of her complete lack of boundaries, her willingness to experiment, and her ravenous sexual appetite.

I've had my fair share of illicit affairs with female flight attendants and co-pilots, but none of them were interesting enough to be granted a second fuck by yours truly, let alone be courted or considered for a long-term relationship. But the woman who's filled so many pages with delicate calligraphy and salacious words deserves my full attention. She's certainly maintained it well past the time I closed the cover of her journal—again and again.

Imagining how her naiveté was gradually—and most willingly—robbed from her was simply... enthralling. She's been haunting my wet dreams.

Now, every time I see an unknown stewardess, I wonder if *she*'s the one.

After many conversations with Bob over the past months during our overseas flights, I've come to share some of her journal entries with him. He agrees that I need to locate her. If not for the airline's sake or to satisfy my personal curiosity, then for the mere reason that I could stop obsessing about her and resume paying attention to my actual job: piloting giant aircrafts and safely getting passengers from point A to point B.

The following short stories record my obsession toward her. There are ten in total. Each installment contains my mystery stewardess's original journal entries for a specific location, followed by my own experiences in trying to track her down. You'll discover what (and whom) I did in an effort to identify and locate my stewardess based on the clues she's left in her diary. You can read the episodes in any order, but they'll probably make more sense if you start from the beginning and follow along as I attempt to find her.

And, just to be clear, these stories should *not* land in the hands of any prude or underage person. Some are just romantic, sensual, or highly erotic, while others are immoral, perverse, and possibly even illegal in some parts of the world.

Ah, the things I'll do to this mystery stewardess when I finally encounter her in the flesh!

I'm hard just thinking about it...

Yours truly,

Capt. Charlie
Undisclosed Airline

PART ONE

THE STEWARDESS'S
ENTRIES

I SMILED at my boy-toy Matt when I pulled my duty-free cart next to row 44.

I reached up and toggled the call button off. Sitting next to Matt, an older gentleman held the in-flight magazine opened on the perfume page. He was clearly the one who'd pressed the service button.

"Do you think my wife will like this sample box?" he asked me, pointing at a Dior variety boxset.

"I don't know your wife and her taste in perfumes, but this particular assortment's quite popular. And I'm sure she'll absolutely love the thoughtful gesture."

The silver-haired man smiled at me. "Perfect, I'll take it. Now let me find my credit card," he said before digging through the seat pocket in front of him. A few seconds later, he unbuckled and got up, so I moved my cart forward to clear the aisle. It seemed the man had placed his wallet in the overhead compartment.

While waiting, I glanced at Matt, who was tucking a strand of his long brown hair behind his ear. He winked at me, his chocolate eyes disrobing me from within. I couldn't believe how handsome he looked... and how lucky I was to have him with me right now. But maybe it wasn't all luck. I'd learned from our planned Mexican getaway. This time, I'd made sure Matt wasn't going to cancel on me: I'd gotten him a seat on *my* flight. But our plane wasn't going fast enough. We'd be landing in Dublin in less than an hour. But still, that was too long. Couldn't I already be naked next to him? Hell... *over* and *under* him as well? The more positions, the better.

"There it is," the older man said, a brown leather wallet in hand.

I opened the cart drawer where the perfumes were stored and found what he wanted. After taking the credit card he offered, I processed the transaction, then handed the gentleman his card back along with a duty-free bag that contained his wife's gift. *How thoughtful of him. Can't say anyone's ever bought me duty-free souvenirs, but I can buy my own. Come to think of it, pretty little trinkets and perfume bottles are at the bottom of my wish list. I'd much rather enjoy a sensual getaway with a tall hottie like Matt. Collecting experiences is much better than accumulating objects.* Especially when these experiences brought me to the brink of earthly pleasures.

I smiled at the elderly passenger and Matt before making my way back to stow the duty-free cart in its rightful location, lost in my own thoughts. When Matt contacted me to say that things were through with his ex, I couldn't have been more pleased. If there was a guy whom I wouldn't mind having a string of one-night stands with, it was Matt. We'd known each other for over six months now, since his brief stint as a flight attendant. I always knew he wasn't relationship material, but that aspect of his personality was fine with me now; I wasn't looking for love anymore—*at least, I think I've convinced myself of it.*

I couldn't think of anyone better to share a long weekend with at a secluded, one-of-a-kind Irish castle—according to the online reviews I'd found.

I'm sure our free time will be spent having sex more than taking in the scenery.

And I was fine with that.

I could enjoy the beautiful Irish landscape some other time.

CUSTOMS CLEARED and our small overnight bags duly stashed in our rental car, Matt closed the trunk—or the boot, as he called it.

"Want to drive?" he asked, keys in hand.

I had no issues driving in general, but couldn't say I felt super comfortable doing it on the left side of the road.

"I can if you want to close your eyes and rest, but—"

"Rest? I was asking to be polite. I'd much rather drive! It's been a while since I drove on the *correct* side of the road," he said, a sarcastic smile on his lips. "This little sports car should be great craic to maneuver around winding roads."

I got on my tip-toes and kissed him. *How I loved Irish accents... Or any accent for that matter.* "It's all yours!"

Being spoiled and letting men treat me like a princess was quite a pleasant change. *I should have started years ago.*

As we headed west out of Dublin, embarking on our three-hour drive toward the secluded castle, we finally left the urban scenery and the green rolling hills gradually began to expand in all directions. The odd rock wall or herd of sheep broke the emerald color scheme every now and then. The gray sky hung low, threatening to rip open, but it appeared that good ole Irish luck was on our side.

AFTER VEERING off the road and following the signage, we finally made it to the castle. The large stone building was well kept, at least judging by the beautiful edges and trimmed trees lining the driveway. Lush climbing plants covered the castle's tallest tower; they'd almost successfully camouflaged the grey stones to match their surrounding green environment.

Matt kept driving until we reached a sign that identified the main entrance. Thunder roared the instant he turned off the ignition. We got out of the car and grabbed our carry-on bags, leaving our vehicle parked in front of the entrance. Although we both ran to the door, our excitement to get out of the rain came to a halt when we saw the sign telling us to knock and wait.

My boy-toy rapped the heavy iron knocker, whose ring must have been nearly a foot wide and about an inch thick. We waited. Like a true gentleman, Matt left me standing under the deep, pointed doorway made of stones while he got soaked; his beautiful hair was no longer flowing and wavy, but now dripping wet.

"Don't be silly, there's room for the two of us," I said.

"No, best keep you and our bags dry." His head nodded toward the two carry-on bags stacked next to me on the threshold. A smile then grew on his lips. "I'll get out of these wet clothes the second we're in the room—"

With a creaky squeal, the heavy wooden door opened behind me. A tuxedoed butler let us in. While his clothes reminded me of Michael Caine's outfit in *Batman*, the young lad's face looked a lot more like Liam Hemsworth from *The Hunger Games*. *How strange to see a real live manservant, especially one that was in his early twenties and sexy.*

Matt finally left the rain and joined me as I walked into the building.

"Welcome to our castle," the butler said while I

looked up and around, taking in the vast entrance hall. The stone walls had been painted in white, and beautiful large tapestries hung to cover most of the available space. Above our heads, dark wooden beams met in pointed arcs at least three stories higher than our level. A large electrical chandelier hung about ten feet above our heads in the center of the room. Around us, a few pieces of humongous wooden furniture sparsely decorated with wild flowers adorned the space.

"Wow!" I couldn't help but say aloud.

"First time?" the butler asked.

I nodded and so did Matt, who was now holding both of our bags, looking toward the reception desk.

"I'm sure you'll have a wonderful stay," the manservant said, looking at the both of us. "Do you have any luggage you'd like me to take care of?"

"No, we're good, thank you. But what should I do with the car?" Matt asked, holding the keys in the air.

"I'll take care of it for you, then I'll leave the keys with Jessica. Why don't you go ahead and check yourselves in?" The butler said, his hand pointing toward the reception area that Matt had been staring at. "She'll take great care of you."

"Thank you," I said before following Matt.

The second I set eyes on Jessica, I understood why Matt had so intently been staring that way. The beautiful red-headed woman wore her hair in a ponytail tied on one side, reminding me of 80s fashion, but her green eyes, pale skin, and bright red lips screamed *cougar in bed*. Her outfit certainly supported that theory. She wore what would best be described as a French maid outfit, with a very, very deep scoop neck. Her breasts were pushed up, their white flesh bulging out of the outfit. So much of her chest was exposed that her nipples had to start less than half an inch from where the lacy white border ended. A little bit of black fabric puffed around her tiny shoulders. The short sleeves ended on her slender arms in a lacy border that echoed the pattern of the tiny white apron that hung around her waist. I couldn't see her legs from where we stood, but I was willing to bet the bottom of her body matched the top. So far, the castle staff could have been picked right out of an issue of GQ magazine.

"Hello, *Dia dhuit!* Welcome to the ▮▮▮▮▮▮▮ Castle."

3:10 P.M.

ONCE JESSICA HAD REGISTERED us and upgraded us from the *breakfast-only* to the *full-meal plan*, which she highly recommended—the same recommendation that had been made by every online reviewer—she assigned us our room for the weekend. Our old-fashioned metal keys in hand, we stepped off of the thick *Welcome* mat we were standing on and turned around before heading toward the metal spiral staircase located at the back of the room.

At the foot of the stairs, next to a brass luggage trolley, stood two beautiful women, one tall blonde and one curvy brunette, also wearing matching French maid outfits. The bottoms of their uniforms left as little to the imagination as the top did. The puffy black fabric flared out for about a foot from the waist down. Then a couple of inches of white crinoline poked out all around the hem. Sheer black stockings covered their legs, the darker band at the top was visible just below the end of the crinoline. "Hello, my name's Kate," said the brunette closest to the luggage trolley as we got within about three feet of them. "I'll take your bags and bring them to your room if that's alright?"

Matt, who was holding his bag over his left shoulder and rolling my carry-on behind him, seemed to consider it for a second, but the narrowness of the staircase probably made him change his mind. He placed both of our bags on the trolley, which Kate then pushed out of the room. The clicks of her high heels and the thumping noises of the wheels as they rolled over the ceramic tiles faded out as we watched her disappear with our bags into a small hallway.

The blonde woman then addressed us. "I'm Chloe. If you'll follow me, I'll take you to your room now."

I nodded. She turned around, then started her way up the stairs.

"After you," said Matt with a fake curtsy.

I grabbed a hold of the black metal railway and started climbing, then looked up to see where I was going. Chloe was already ten steps ahead of me, her puffy crinoline bottom swaying as she made her way up, forcing my eyes to inadvertently turn into heat-seeking missiles aiming for her lacy white panties. They covered less than a third of her butt cheeks. I looked down at Matt, who met my eyes. He had a wide grin on his lips. He nodded toward the maid above us. I smiled and raised my shoulders at him, then resumed climbing. I wouldn't be giving him a show of my own since I'd changed into jeans and a light V-neck sweater after landing. *Too bad for him.* And I was certainly happy to be wearing flat shoes. I don't know how these maids could walk all day on uneven tiles and narrow metal staircases in that kind of footwear!

Once the three of us had finished climbing, Chloe smiled at us and headed to the right, down a wide hallway lined with large oil paintings.

"Feel free to explore every nook and cranny of this castle," she said as I admired the work of the artists.

The first painting was of a large woman eating grapes in a deep green garden, naked, lying on her side. The second one displayed a man with a woman kneeling in front a him while he kissed another woman standing next to him, all of them naked, save for the top hat worn by the man. *Hmmm. Am I just horny, or is this place 'one-of-a-kind' for a specific reason?*

Matt wrapped his arm around my waist and whispered in my ear, "My, my! What kind of place did you book for us? They certainly know how to put people in the mood. Can't wait to get you naked—"

"Consider this castle your home for the entire weekend," Chloe said as she veered left into a smaller corridor. "Ab-so-lu-tely nothing is out of bounds here."

A light beep sounded and I turned to look in the direction the noise had come from. An elevator door opened and out came Kate with the luggage trolley.

"Just in time," said Chloe.

I turned to face her, and she walked into the tall wooden door she'd just opened. Matt and I followed her into the room.

Chloe smiled at the both of us. "This is your bedroom. Remember that the entire staff is at your beck and call, for any and all of your needs." She pointed to a phone on one of the nightstands.

"Press 0 and you'll reach Jessica or whoever is manning the front desk."

Just as she finished speaking, Kate rolled our luggage into the room, then placed each of the bags on a large wooden bench at the end of the four-post, king-sized bed, which could have come from a princess story with its sheer burgundy curtains. They covered the top of the bed then had been loosely tied around the posts.

"Should I unpack your bags for you?" she offered.

I shook my head. "No, there's no need. But thank you."

Matt dug into his pant pocket to retrieve his wallet then walked toward Kate.

"Fine," she said. "I won't unpack your bags, but I'll light a fire. We wouldn't want the two of you to catch a cold." Kate reached up to place a strand of Matt's wet hair behind his ear. She smiled and winked at him before turning away and heading toward the sizable fireplace across the room from the bed.

Am I imagining things or was she flirting with him?

Matt turned to look at me, his face scrunched up. *Guess I'm not the only confused one here.*

A creak then sounded on my right. The other

maid had opened up the large wardrobe on the outside wall. "We offer an assortment of dresses and tuxedos for our guests in the event they forgot to pack formal evening wear. Based on the size of your bags, I assume you may need to borrow from what you'll find in here. Like I said, feel free to open drawers, wardrobes, and whatever you find. Poke around. Everything here is clean and ready for our guests." Her right hand motioned toward the fireplace as she finished speaking.

I turned to see what she was pointing at. Her words suddenly took on an entirely new meaning.

Kate's body was folded in half at the hips, her arms were busy arranging the firewood in the fireplace, but what drew my focus—and probably Matt's as well—was Kate's naked ass and pussy, exposed in the midst of her crinoline.

Matt's arm wrapped around my waist, and he bent down to whisper in my ear. "Is this an early birthday present for me?"

I looked at him. His chocolate eyes simmered with hope. I shook my head. "No idea what's happening."

And with that, the faint sounds of small branches lighting up reached my ears, followed by the clicks of Kate's heels. She was heading our way with a large, innocent smile on her face.

Matt unwrapped his arm from me and handed Kate a five-euro bill he'd previously retrieved from his wallet. "Thank you," he said.

Kate took the money and waved it in the air toward Chloe, who walked over and took it from her hand.

"We're sorry," said Kate. She turned her attention to Matt and brought one finger down the center of his wet shirt. "We... don't... accept... tips..." Her hand was still going down, slowly but definitely. She passed his leather belt. "Not in cash, anyway..." Her sliding finger turned into a full-hand grab of Matt's genitals.

I was about to protest, but felt something slide into the front of my V-neck. I looked down. Matt's folded five-euro bill was resting in the tight groove of my pushed-up cleavage.

"What the—"

Chloe locked her lips onto mine, one of her hands behind the nape of my neck and the other wrapped around my left hand, which she brought to her own breast. She pulled down her scoop neck and pushed my hand onto one of her soft, squishy but firm breasts.

No bra. I felt the built-in wire in the dress's stretchy fabric on the back of my hand. Chloe pushed me onto the bed, her lips hungrier than a starving porn actress. Her tongue parted my lips before exploring my mouth. I let her but couldn't return the enthusiasm. I turned to look at Matt, which forced Chloe to move her kisses to my neck, then to the exposed skin of my cleavage.

Matt's head tilted back, his eyes locked on the ceiling, his mouth agape. His pants were crumbled around his ankles, his hands wrapped around the brunette's head. She had knelt in front of him and had gotten busy sucking his dick. He started moaning. His hips began moving back and forth toward Kate, forcing her to take all of him inside her mouth.

"We don't accept tips in Euros," Chloe said to me as she sat up on my hips, her legs folded around me. "Kate likes full-lengths, and I... like other types of tips," she said before lifting my sweater.

I'd come here for a sensual weekend. I hadn't planned for it to involve people other than Matt... *but why not?*

I raised my arms and lifted my back off from the dark burgundy comforter, letting her pull my sweater above my head. She tossed it to the side. Her hands then reached behind my back and unclasped my bra. A second later, with my arms cleared of the straps, she tossed the unneeded lacy garment toward my sweater. Chloe's hands brought my breasts together, massaging them forcefully before focusing her attention on my nipples. She twisted and squeezed them before getting closer to me and sucking on one of them. She moaned, the sound partially obstructed by my breast as her lips gently nibbled on my nipple.

Matt's groans started getting louder. I knew him well enough to know he was about to come.

I looked at him; his gaze had turned to Chloe and me. My eyes met his as he reached orgasm. His hips jerked forward and he pulled Kate's head closer, not even giving her the option to retract.

He let out a loud grunt and closed his eyes. Kate forced her head back a few seconds later, then slowly got up. She smiled at him before wiping some of Matt's come from her chin with her index finger.

"Welcome to our castle. I hope you'll enjoy your stay," Kate said.

And just like that, Chloe got off of me and left me half-naked on the bed as I watched both maids walk away. But just before they reached the door, Chloe turned around and said, "Dinner will be served at seven in the main dining hall. Formalwear, please. You may want to get some rest before then. You'll need it."

The door creaked as they closed it behind them.

Matt took off his shoes, then kicked off his pants and underwear before walking my way. In a swift motion, he removed his wet shirt, exposing his six-pack abs just as he reached the bed.

"How did a five-euro note lead to this?" my gorgeous, naked Adonis asked me as he approached the bed.

I sat up. "Disappointed?"

Matt raised his shoulders. A half-smile on his lips, he asked, "What would twenty euros have gotten me you think?"

I slapped him on the ass. "Probably the same..." I inhaled deeply as I pulled him closer to me. "Matt, I didn't get my happy ending... Would you mind giving me a hand?"

He pushed me back onto the bed and undid my pants.

"Can I give you a tongue instead?"

MY CHEEKS ROSY with post-orgasm glee, I walked butt naked toward the en-suite bath.

"I think I'll do like they said and relax. I feel like taking a bath," I said to Matt as I opened the en-suite door.

Whoever had decorated the room had done so with women patrons in mind. Heavy flowery curtains decorated the window. Three beautiful ceramic vases were overflowing with fresh-cut white roses, baby's breath, and assorted green leaves. Two sets of plush white towels hung on a rack in front of the window. Other than the thickness of the window frame—which had to be at least a foot deep —there were no signs of being in a stone castle.

The walls were flat, flawless, and had been painted in a light shade of salmon. A large and ornate gold mirror decorated the main wall. This bathroom had everything one would expect and more: a modern pedestal sink, a four-legged bathtub with brass fittings, a large corner shower, a vanity table with a small mirror and a padded, armless Victorian chair upholstered in a flowery pattern that matched the curtains, a modern low-flow toilet, and even a bidet! Behind the bathroom door had been hung two soft bathrobes. I reached and touched the fabric. *Decadently soft.*

I wrapped myself in one of them then stepped out of the room to look at Matt.

He was sitting up in bed, remote in hand, his naked lower body tucked under the covers.

"The tub's huge. You want to have a bath with me?" I asked.

"Nah, I found a game I'd like to watch: Republic of Ireland's playing Belarus."

"Aren't you cold from getting soaked earlier?"

He shrugged. "I'm good. The fire's hot and the sheets are keeping me warm."

"Enjoy the game then," I said as I returned to the bathroom.

I turned on the faucets, adjusted the

temperature, and filled the tub with warm water. An assortment of bath products had been stacked on the vanity table. I opted for the jasmine-scented bath salts.

Once my bath was ready, I lowered my body into the perfumed water and rested my back against the slanted end of the tub. I closed my eyes and relaxed, inhaling the delicious aroma and letting the fizzy salts caress my thighs as they dissolved.

"IRELAND WON," Matt whispered in my ear, waking me up.

He was sitting on the vanity chair that he'd pulled closer to the tub. Seemed he'd also given in to the temptation to wrap himself in a soft, plush bathrobe. One of his arms was immersed in the tub. I smiled at him as I felt his finger tease me from under the water.

He bent toward me and kissed me. His mouth nibbled my lips, then his tongue probed and twisted in my mouth. I wrapped one of my hands around the back of his neck. His hair had dried up.

A few seconds later, he pulled away.

"Your water's cooled off," he said. "Want me to

give you a massage?" His eyebrows lifted and he smiled. "I found massage oil in the nightstand drawer... among other things."

I was unsure what else he'd discovered, but Matt's expert hands on my skin sounded divine right now. And he could continue tickling my pussy anywhere.

I kissed him again. "Sounds like a great idea."

After he pulled his arm out of the water, I got up, then stepped out of the tub. Matt stood up as well, then extended his arms to offer the bathrobe I'd left resting on the back of the chair.

4:55 P.M.

LYING flat on my stomach on the very comfortable bed, my head facing the TV and fireplace, I asked Matt to pass me the remote. The sports channel didn't offer the most relaxing soundtrack—at least not for me. I flipped through the channels, trying to find one with soft music. I felt Matt's weight on my butt, the warmth of his naked thighs against my hips. He squirted massage oil in his hands then rubbed them together before touching my back. I continued flipping through the channels, glancing at various options along the way: news, movies, cartoons, more sports, porn... Seemed the castle had opted for the most complete cable package.

Matt's hands rubbed my neck and shoulders,

loosening knots I didn't realize I had. I stopped my channel flicking for a second to enjoy his handy work. It seemed I had reached a black and white channel. The footage moved sideways slowly, displaying stone walls with strings of garlic; pots and pans hung from various hooks. Then, a tall wooden shelving unit came into view. It held four large old fashioned clay containers, three Italian coffee makers, and a bunch of larger pots. Half a dozen French maids seemed hard at work, chopping vegetables and tenderizing meat on an oversized island in the center of the room. *A security camera in the kitchen?*

A few feet from the busy maids, a tuxedoed man was stabbing a large brick of ice with a pick to break it into small chunks. The camera kept rotating. It now showcased another French maid stirring a large pot on a stove. *Soup for dinner tonight?* Then, as the kitchen camera reached the end of its wide angle, another French maid appeared—a patisserie chef based on the rolling pin and the amount of flour spread out on the surface in front of her. But her humongous breasts were no longer confined by her uniform; they bounced and brushed back and forth against the flour while a tall, dark, short-curly-haired man in jeans and T-shirt pounded her from behind, his hands on her hips, the bottom of her dress bunched up in front of him.

The camera kept rotating and slowly returned to the maid who was stirring soup then headed back the other way.

Once my agape mouth returned to its normal position, I turned to Matt. "Did you see this?"

"Hell yeah! They weren't kidding about doing what the fuck we wanted." He grabbed the remote from my hands. "I wonder what else... or *whom* else we can see on camera..."

"You think it's live? Or pre-recorded?"

Matt raised his shoulders, his mouth turned upside down. He flipped to the next channel.

More black and white footage populated the screen, but this time, various straps, shackles, whips, and other assorted tools hung from the stone walls. A large chandelier with lit candle sticks dangled low in the room. So low in fact that a six-foot tall person like Matt could easily reach up and replace the candles... Or use them to do whatever. As the camera rotated, I wondered what I'd see in this room. *A woman with one of these ball-thingies in her mouth? A man wearing a leather outfit with metal spikes?* But no, the room was empty.

"I wonder where this is?" Matt asked before flipping to the next channel.

This time, the shot was fixed, the security camera wasn't moving at all since there was no need. It was a small laundry room featuring a modern washer, a dryer, and a half-dozen laundry baskets in front of the machines. In the far corner, several drying lines had been strung, currently covered by uniforms, underwear, and other items of clothing. Yet another gorgeous French maid sat on the top-loading washer. Hard to tell with the black and white image, but her hair was either blonde or light red, tied up in a braid whose tip rested on her breast. Her eyes were beady and dark. But what was obvious was her enjoyment of the spin cycle. Her entire body vibrated along with the machine. One of her legs hung nonchalantly in front of her while the other was folded, her foot resting on the top of the washer. Her panties had gone AWOL but she'd replaced them with a dildo whose full length she slowly pushed and pulled out of her. Her other hand was resting on the top of her thigh, two of her fingers busily rubbing her clit.

"We need laundry done?" Matt asked. "Maybe I can go and help that poor maid."

I took my attention away from the TV screen

and turned to look at my boy-toy. He'd already begun stroking his erect shaft. "Seems like someone's ready for action," I said.

I pushed my ass up in the air, nudging him to get his hips off of me and start poking me where I wanted: deep down into my wet pussy.

"Can I do you in the ass, babe?"

AFTER BROWSING through the selection of evening dresses offered in the armoire, I opted for one that fit me best: a long, one-shoulder black dress with embroidered details. The main part of the dress was made of solid, silky black fabric with detailed lace patterns on the shoulder and down the front. It contained vertical and semi-circular wires like a built-in corset of sort, serving to keep the dress in position, slim my appearance, and push up my breasts. Exactly what I wanted from an evening gown. Once the dress got to mini-skirt length, the solid fabric turned into a sheer lacy pattern that matched the flowers on the top. That see-through section was slit down the left leg in the front, allowing for a comfortable stroll. I picked a three-inch black sandal from the armoire's selection and put on my set of silver looped earrings to finish my outfit.

I looked at myself in the full-length mirror lining the inside of the wardrobe. I pivoted and noticed the unsightly lines my panties made through the bottom of the dress. I took them off and looked at my reflection again.

What a dress! I should ask if I can buy it when we check out.

"You look hot!" said Matt as he came out of the bathroom, his ocean-scented cologne reaching my nostrils before I even turned to look at him. His tuxedo fit him impeccably; his hair brushed the shoulders of his jacket, making him look like an actor on Oscar night. He walked toward me, hunger in his eyes.

"You think we have time for a quickie?" he asked, one of his hands reaching into the slit of my dress and exploring my groin. "A lady commando! Now that's exciting."

A quick glance at his tented pants proved he meant what he'd just said.

The hands of the gold-framed clock on the wall indicated it was already 6:55 p.m.

I was unzipping Matt's pants just as a man's deep voice echoed above us: "Ladies and gents. This announcement is for all patrons who are joining us for dinner. The first service will commence in five minutes. Please join us in the great hall. We appreciate your punctuality."

"Guess that means no?" Matt said before letting out a sigh.

"Come on, we don't want to be rude and show up late."

He looked down at his pants. "Give me a minute. I can't walk out like this..."

I giggled. "Really?"

His eyes sent question marks my way.

"Come on... Given what we've seen so far in this place, nobody will mind." I wrapped my hands around his shoulders and stole a kiss from him.

A few seconds later, we headed out of the room and descended to the main floor in the elevator I'd seen Kate use a few hours earlier.

7:00 P.M.

A MUSCULAR, crew-cut blond man in a tuxedo offered us each a flute of champagne as we entered the great hall.

The room had to be at least one hundred feet across. A dozen couples mingled, creating a light background of high-pitched giggles, laughter, and chit-chat that echoed in the three-story-tall space. Some couples stood by the large lit-up fireplace while others sat on the oversized leather furniture that lined the gray stone walls. Although a vast diversity of skin tones and body types were portrayed, one thing was common among all: everyone was dressed to the nines, as though attending a glamorous event reserved for the rich and famous.

Draped in white linen at the center of the hall, a large rectangular dining table commanded the room, raised on a platform along with its chairs. *How did they manage to place the ornate floral arrangements in the middle of such a large table?* Someone had had to walk on top of the table cloth to do so. I counted sixteen chairs at the table.

"Look at this guy," Matt whispered in my ear, pointing to a brown-haired man chatting with a petite, strawberry-blonde woman.

I finished my sip and lowered my glass. "You know him?"

"No, but wasn't he the guy?"

"What guy?"

He lifted his eyebrows. "In the kitchen? Security footage?"

I looked at the hair on his nape: little curls that kinked out.

"You're right!"

Matt pulled me by the elbow and we walked over to introduce ourselves.

I recognized French when we got within ear shot.

"*Bonsoir*, good evening," the petite woman said to us as we approached. Her thin lips framed the cutest smile. She wore a burgundy, spaghetti-strapped dress that embraced her miniature curves. The large nipples of her tiny perky breasts poked in the front. The hem of her dress ended diagonally, showcasing her athletic calves. *One would be hard-pressed to find fat on her body.* The man accompanying her—Jean-Michel he called himself—was already conversing with Matt. His charismatic smile complemented his clean-shaven, square jaw. He winked at me as he wrapped his arm around his wife's waist.

"It is our second time here. And you?" Jean-Michel asked Matt.

"First-time," he replied.

"Ah, I remember our first hour here last time." Jean-Michel inhaled deeply, his eyes looking up as though he was reminiscing. "Surprising place, no?"

While Matt and the handsome Frenchman got to know each other, I conversed in French with the woman whose name turned out to be Lucie. She and her husband of twenty years had come here to celebrate their wedding anniversary this weekend. *They don't look their age at all!* Not a speck of gray could be seen in Jean-Michel's lush dark hair and not even a hint of crow's feet registered around the corners of Lucie's eyes. *How can people married for twenty years still look like they're in their early thirties at most? White lies? Or do they take great care of their bodies?*

Once our social niceties were over with, Lucie grabbed my elbow and dragged me away from Matt and her husband, toward the closest waiter.

She grabbed my empty glass and placed it on the waiter's tray before helping herself to two new flutes of champagne. She handed me one. *"Après le repas, tu verras, les gens vont bien s'amuser."* She raised her glass and offered a cheers. *"Santé!"*

"Santé!" I repeated before clinking my glass against hers, wondering what she meant by the expected after-dinner fun.

"Tu pourrais venir nous rejoindre plus tard? Moi et mon mari? Chambre numéro 6?"

While I pondered her offer for me to join her and her husband in room 6 after dinner tonight, she motioned for me to follow her.

We headed toward a towering David-esque ice sculpture on a long table. It was similar to the famous Michelangelo's stone sculpture, except that the ice artist responsible for this piece of art had given David a large boner. Next to him, on a bed of crushed ice rested fresh oysters and a three-tiered platform overflowing with pink prawns. A row of condiments were at the ready: salt, a bottle of Tabasco, fresh lime quarters, and a small bowl filled with red, chunky sauce.

I thought about her offer while enjoying another bubbly sip. "*Avec ou sans Matt?*" I asked her, wondering if she also wanted Matt to come along.

She grabbed a juicy oyster and brought it up to her lips. "*Toi seulement,*" she replied, her frank eyes steady, almost as though a mental duel was about to begin. She tilted her unadulterated oyster, maintaining eye contact with me before noisily slurping all of its content. With her pointy tongue, she licked her lips to suck up some of the liquid that had escaped before tossing the empty shell on the platter where other empty ones had already been piled. *Looks like it's not just her husband who's looking for an extra woman?*

A light bell chimed, and I turned to look at yet another tuxedoed man. This one was bald and tall, his skin as dark as the night. He cranked *handsome* to a whole new level. He cleared his throat before addressing us. "Ladies and gents, please have a seat. Make new friends and mingle."

I recognized his voice from the earlier announcement.

"*Et puis?*" Lucie asked me, prompting me to provide a response.

I looked at her handsome husband in the distance, still chatting with Matt. *A threesome with one handsome Frenchman and another woman? That would be a new experience. Maybe figure out if French people were the best lovers as some of them claimed.* "Why not? *Oui.*"

After telling me she had to share the news with her husband, she excused herself and walked away, leaving me standing alone. Everyone around me had started making their way to the table. I looked at Matt across the room. A short cappuccino-skinned woman whose long black hair reached her waist was already dragging my Matt to the table, her arm intertwined with his at the elbow. Matt lifted his free hand in the air and pulsed his shoulders up while looking at me.

Guess I'm on my own for dinner.

And just as the thought occurred to me, a pale-skinned, red-headed man approached me.

"I'm Kenny. Would ya like to chat with me over dinner?"

7:15 P.M.

I JOINED Kenny at the dining room table. He chose a seat to my right. Before I could sit myself down, a tuxedoed waiter gentlemanly approached the chair for me. On my left sat a plump black woman in a beautiful pearly-white gown. She smiled and nodded at me before turning her attention to the guest on her left, a tall brunette with her hair wrapped in a chignon.

I looked at Kenny just as one of the gorgeous maids was placing a small bowl of pale green liquid in front of me. The castle's staff worked in perfect unison, serving all guests within seconds of each other.

46

"Dig in!" Kenny said as he covered his lap with a white napkin.

I dipped my silverware into the steamy liquid and brought a spoonful to my lips: delicious cream of broccoli. I was starving and hadn't realized it.

"So, ya like our castle here?" Kenny asked between spoonfuls.

"Gotta say, I didn't quite know what I was getting myself into..."

He nodded, a large smile on his lips, which created two cute dimples on his freckled cheeks. "When did ya arrive?"

"This afternoon." I dipped my spoon into what remained of my soup.

"Ya're in for a whale of a time," he said, his red bushy eyebrows going up a couple of times.

"So, you're from around here?" I asked him after finishing my soup and tapping my napkin on my lips.

"Sure look it. What about ya? What's the story?"

We continued on with social niceties and chit-chatted about nothing of importance while the perfectly-choreographed service continued. The next courses consisted of poached salmon with a side of baby potatoes then a small tossed salad with a raspberry vinaigrette. Two tuxedoed men constantly circled the table as we ate, ensuring every guest's wine glass remained full throughout the meal.

By the time the plates of lamb cutlets had been cleared from the table, the conversation had gotten pretty loud, which wasn't unexpected considering the amount of alcohol everyone was ingesting.

After a quick and polite apology, my dinner friend turned his attention to the lady on his right, a short, spiked-hair blonde, therefore freeing me to look around without guilt. I saw Matt six seats away from me, chatting up the cappuccino-skinned woman. The whiteness of her teeth contrasted vividly against her thick red lips. Just as I was trying to guess her age, her eyes widened and her entire body jolted, her back straightened, and her hands reached below the table. Then, a second later, Matt's body pulsed up; his eyes lurched down at his groin. A groan from Kenny on my right brought my attention to him. But he didn't appear surprised at all, his dimples had reappeared on both sides of his wide smile. His eyes were closed.

What the heck is going on here?

Then, I felt it too.

I looked down at my hips and saw a bulge form

from under the table cloth in front of me. A hand with bright red nails brushed up my lap, coming out from underneath the cloth for a few seconds as it pushed the bottom of my dress out of the way, bunching up the fabric and pushing it off to the side. I lifted my ass for a second, just so I'd be more comfortable, then I slid myself down, closer to the mystery woman below the table in front of me.

I looked around me once more. The waiting staff had all disappeared. The room had gotten quiet, all conversations having abruptly ended. My mystery woman proceeded to part my legs wide enough to lodge herself between my thighs. Soft silky hair brushed against my skin, two hands and a tongue slowly made their way up my inner thighs. A warm breath blew onto my genitals. Wet fingers slid down my pussy, then back up, stroking my lips without poking me... at first.

Then, the warm and moist air of her breath blew harder onto my clit, her wet tongue twirled around it before the woman's mouth nuzzled into my pussy, forcing my thighs to part even more. Her agile tongue licked and sucked on my clit, her fingers still stroked my lips, faster and faster, squeezing my folds tighter. Then her wet finger slid into my pussy. Another finger soon joined it. They rubbed and tapped upward, as though feeling their way toward the right spot. A few delicious seconds later, they found it.

A moan escaped my lips. Then another... and another. I couldn't control myself. Her tongue and lips left my clit, then she tongue-fucked me as her fingers polished my wet button. I brought one of my hands down to keep my lips parted. My other hand went to my heart, as though its presence there could prevent it from exploding out of my chest. Her expert tongue kept going. Then it was again replaced by her fingers. I could hear my own moisture as she thrust her digits in and out, quickly. She poked at the exact right spot where I needed to be prodded. My legs quivered. My back arched. My neck fell backward onto the back of my chair as I came. My thighs framed the mystery woman squarely in place as my drenched pussy pulsed out of control around her fingers.

I reopened my eyes once the orgasmic tsunami finished washing over me.

The dinner conversations had morphed into a cacophony of moans, groans, and calls to diverse deities. Everybody was receiving or had just finished receiving premium head, at least based on every patrons' facial expressions. Some were grabbing on to the table, a woman had pushed down her dress and was twisting her bare nipples, another pushed over her wine glass, which landed in a clang over her empty tea cup and plate.

I looked down at Kenny's lap just as the black-haired woman who was sucking his cock came out for air. I got to see his masterpiece: his bright white dick had to be at least ten inches long. And who knew if there was another inch or two that remained hidden within his Irish red carpet.

My dishes slid to the left, along with the table cloth. I couldn't catch my plate before it crashed on the stone floor, breaking into a thousand pieces. The black woman next to me had—probably inadvertently—pulled on the table cloth. Her mouth was agape. Her hands were wrapped around a dark-haired person nuzzled in her groin.

"God, yeeesss!" she screamed.

THE WAITING staff trickled back in the room in the moments that followed.

While a tuxedoed waiter refilled my wine glass, a French maid appeared out of thin air with a broom and tray. The red-headed woman bent down to sweep away my broken dishes, her panty-less, bold crotch staring at me a mere six inches from my face. Her light musky scent reached my nostrils, and she shook her booty, as though inviting my fingers to tease her while she worked. Blame it on the wine, or blame it on the fabulous head I'd just gotten, but I couldn't resist. I reached to touch her. She moaned the instant my fingers came in contact with her wet labia. She was warm. She was dripping wet.

She backed up ever so slightly, pushing herself onto my fingers, as though urging me to move them, to probe her, and explore her inner folds. My digits made circular motions around her wet opening before dipping into her. Her juices dripped down my hand. She backed up some more, forcing my fingers deeper into her. The black woman on my left got up, walked up to the cleanup maid, and started kissing her. The maid's body unfolded as she straightened up. The maid let go of her broom and tray, her hands reaching up to the black woman's face as their kiss increased in intensity.

I hesitated for a second. Unsure what to do.

"Keep going," I heard Kenny's voice say from behind me.

I turned and saw him looking at the three of us. He had moved his chair sideways. He was now facing us, stroking his humongous naked shaft. A few feet behind him, the spiked-hair lady was kneeling, sucking on one of the waiters. The whole room had seemingly agreed upon a free-form orgy of sorts.

I resumed finger-fucking the maid's pussy. I brought my face to her soft and firm butt cheeks. I kissed their plush roundness, I caressed their contours. My cadence increased, following the maid's hips' rocking motions. Her hand then suddenly lurched to her ass, parting her cheeks and exposing her anus. I let the tip of my tongue go down her crevice until I could tickle her opening.

I felt another hand come near her pussy, touching my fingers, then retracting back toward the maid's clit. The maid's moans got louder. Her inner walls were clenching around my fingers. I thrust deeper and deeper into her. Her wetness lubricated my fingers so much that I felt the need to insert a third one, then a fourth one so I could fill her soaked and slippery pussy. And just with that, she came, squirting a jet of liquid that streamed down my arm and dripped off of my elbow, onto the stones below.

"Fuck yeah!" Kenny groaned.

ONE OF MOZART'S concertos played in the background while patrons and staff finished up their *activities*—for lack of a more encompassing term. The maid resumed her clean-up duties and walked away with the broken dishes in her tray, as if nothing had happened, save for her own juices running down her leg.

A minute later, I watched Kenny squirt onto the floor about a foot away from me. I felt my pussy twitch. This fuck-fest had yet to include a dick in my pussy. Matt's or someone else's. It didn't matter whose. I just needed to be filled right now. I sipped more wine as I looked around to see whose dick was still at the ready and available.

Unfortunately, my quest terminated abruptly as the handsome black butler rang his bell and announced that dessert would be served in a few minutes.

He would do. That hot, bald butler would certainly have a great dick.

I took a few more sips and waited patiently for the hot butler to announce what 'dessert' would consist of. I looked toward the French couple who had invited me for an after-dinner session. Was their offer still on? Or would 'dinner' have done the trick for them? As though they were reading my mind, both Lucie and Jean-Michel were staring at me. Jean-Michel lifted his wine glass toward me, nodded, then winked. Lucie was biting her lower lip. Her hand went from her mouth to her neck, down to her right breast, which she squeezed while locking eyes with me.

The hot butler rang his bell again before clearing his throat. "Tonight, dessert will be picked at random from this hat. Alternatively, you can grab whatever you like and eat it here or anywhere else, as usual. I will be walking around the table for dessert selection."

And with that, the hot bald butler started with Lucie. She dipped her hand into the hat and retrieved a piece of paper. The butler walked over to the next patron and offered her the hat. The routine continued until he reached me. I smiled at him as I plunged my hand into the hat.

The butler walked away before I could even say a thing.

Gotta work on my pick-up lines. Guess I could have just grabbed him without a word?

I unfolded my mystery dessert, which read:

Treasure hunt: A collection of golden cocks has been hidden in the castle. Find at least three and bring them to the butler or maid of your choice to claim your prize.

I smiled. *Here you go. Butler selected. His dick will be my prize, golden or not.*

"What did ya get?" asked Kenny.

"A treasure hunt. You?"

He nodded with a smile before handing me his sliver of paper, which read:

Jello fight: Pick two staff members and join them in a jello boxing match.

I overheard other people around me

mentioning a "spa evening," "kitchen raid," and "chocolate fondue." Seemed every dessert had its appeal.

The light ring of the bell echoed again in the dining room and the hot butler addressed us again. "Please proceed to claim your dessert, as directed by your slip of paper. Enjoy the rest of your evening."

I pushed my chair back, then slowly got up, realizing that I had drenched my chair. I adjusted my dress, grabbed a last swig of my wine, and headed down the hall on my quest to find golden dicks. I decided to start with the kitchen.

AFTER LOOKING in vain from one cupboard to the next, I headed out through a small door in the back of the kitchen to explore the rest of the castle.

I followed the narrow, sparsely decorated stone hallway. A minute later, displayed under a glass dome in the center of a small wall alcove, I found my first golden dick. A golden vibrator really. It even had an on/off switch. A small push of the button indicated the batteries were charged and ready. My aching pussy urged me to think it over for a second. The girth and length of the golden shaft was enticing, but with so many real live dicks around, it seemed worth my while to do as instructed and claim my preferred butler's real appendage once I collected two more golden dildos.

First prize in hand, I continued down the hallway until I reached a staircase that spiraled down below the ground floor. A few electrical lights illuminated my way. A spa-like aroma of mineral salts grew stronger the deeper I went. The humidity level also kept increasing.

Thirty steps later, I ended up in Shangri-La—at least the way the legendary place presented itself in my mind. The colossal, irregular-shaped room appeared to have been carved out of a natural cave, then enhanced by technology and molded to fit the needs of the castle. A beautiful narrow waterfall gushed out from ground level and fell into the back of the larger basin in front of me. Its surface was calm, save for the waves made by Jessica, the red-headed receptionist, who was swimming out of it. The woman had started to make her way out, each step exposing more of her white skin, her fleshy, hard-nippled breasts, her flat stomach, her trimmed red mons, her long legs... Once fully out of the basin, she turned and headed toward a smaller pond that was already occupied by two of the waiters—Liam-Hemsworth-look-alike was one of them.

He smiled at me as I walked by the smaller pond they sat in, feeling the warmth of the nebulous layer that was evaporating from the water. "Want to join us?" he asked.

A hot tub with two hot butlers... Enticing... But I've got another mission. "Maybe later," I said, waving my golden cock in the air. "I'm collecting my dessert."

"Good luck!" he said with a wink.

If I can't find the hot black butler, I'll come back here.

I FOLLOWED the asymmetrical pathway that outlined the circumference of the room until I found a large wooden door. It opened onto yet another stone passageway, this one lit with flickering candles whose molten white wax dripped along the walls and floor below.

Screams and grunts echoed from farther down the hall. I walked toward the noises. The snap of a whip. A woman's cry. The orders of a man's voice: "Shut up and take it!"

I know this voice.

I hurried my pace, my heart pounding against my chest.

Matt? What are you doing?

I reached the door from which the sounds emanated just as the cries morphed into moans of pleasure and worship.

What the heck?

I peeked through the small barred opening that provided just enough of a tease for voyeurs like myself. *The torture room from the security footage!* Matt was standing in the center of the chamber. He'd donned black leather chaps and a studded leather collar. His head was tilted back, his eyes closed. Like a piston, his hips repeatedly and violently rammed into a cappuccino-skinned woman's ass. Her face was fully covered by a red mask, but her long black hair extruded into a ponytail from an opening in the back of the mask. She rested on all fours, her wrists and ankles bound by large black straps tied to the floor. Her stomach rested on a padded stool, but her breasts hung in front of it, with clips that looked like large clothespins attached to her nipples.

Her moans intensified. She arched her back, her buttocks gyrating in front of him. He slapped her ass then gripped her hips to force himself deeper into her anus, impaling her repeatedly, faster and faster until he pulled out and ejaculated all over her bare, creamed-coffee back.

She yelped, begging for more, but I walked away before finding out what would follow.

Guess I don't really know Matt...

I continued my walk down the dim passageway, shaking my head to repress the recently acquired memories.

Hoping to see something a little less distressing (and hopefully find another golden dick), I pushed open the next door, which had been left slightly ajar.

This room was different and dead quiet. Its decoration stood on the opposite end of the spectrum from what I'd just seen. It reminded me of a British tea house. Small round tables were peppered around the room, covered with lacy white tablecloths and fresh-cut flowers. Each table was surrounded by two or three padded Victorian chairs for guests to sit on and chit-chat. A large fireplace reigned at the center of the wall in front of me. Around it were displayed gorgeous, gold-framed paintings, but instead of the Victorian or medieval portraits I would have expected to find here, each chef-d'oeuvre featured bigger-than-life, overly-detailed genitalia of both varieties. The first one I looked at featured a gargantuan erect cock. The artist had made the skin appear velvety soft and inviting, with shadows that made the huge member appear to come out of the painting. I looked at the next one: a large set of engorged labia upon which reigned a stubby clit. This time, the finish wasn't velvety soft; the paint glistened with the flickers of the fireplace. And just then, as I was about to look at the next large painting, a woman cleared her throat.

I turned around and saw one of the maids standing next to a blank canvas.

"Would you like to become part of our collection?" she asked.

This place keeps on surprising...

"Hmm, I think I'll pass for now," I said before once again waving my gold cock in the air. "I'm looking for a few more of these."

"Ah... Well I had taken one, in the event the evening got boring, but you can have it. I'm sure I'll find someone else to occupy myself with," she said with a smile. Her hand reached down among her painting supplies. She retrieved the golden dick and handed it to me.

After thanking her, I left the room and continued on my quest.

A short stroll down the passageway later, I found another alcove built in the stone wall. I retrieved my final piece of the puzzle from underneath its protective dome. At the base of the glass holder were engraved the following words:

May your hungry pussy eat up my entire weight in gold. Again and again.

My third and final dildo in hand, and a grin brought on to my lips by the castle's attention to prose, I opened the last door at the end of the passageway and found another set of stairs, this one leading up. But strangely, the more steps I climbed, the darker it got. I slowed down, letting my eyes adjust to the darkness. A light feeling of claustrophobia rolled over me the higher I got, as though I was climbing to a dead end.

But no. It wasn't the case.

After my eyes finally adjusted to the darkness I found a square opening at the top of the stairs. The ceiling was really low though, I could touch the wooden surface. *No, not a ceiling,* I realized. A faint light came in all around me. I walked toward it and reached a layer padded with plush cushions. Then a step, then a cloth draping from above.

I crawled out from underneath the surface and saw that I had found the waiters' secret passageway to the "head course" of the meal. The diners had long gone though. I was alone in the great hall and had absolutely no idea where I could find my hot butler so I could claim my prize.

Security camera!

With a plan in mind, I went back to my room. I knew Matt was probably still down in the torture room, inflicting pain to the cappuccino woman, whose cries still resonated in my mind. *She found pleasure in that?*

Once I got in my bedroom, I flicked through the security channels: laundry room, torture room —Matt was still at it, but another woman had joined them, this one with a studded leather outfit. *Argh, that's too much for me.* I continued flicking: the kitchen, the dining room, the reception... *There he is!* He was alone, watching something on a screen.

But I realized all of this running back and forth had kind of dried me up... *Maybe I should warm myself up again.*

I turned on one of my dildos. Its soft burr roared gently in my otherwise quiet room. I sat on the bench at the foot of the bed, looking at my bald black man on TV. He had a remote in hand. Whatever he was watching had probably dulled his interest. I looked at his dark beady eyes on the screen. His tongue moistened his lips, exposing his bright white teeth for a second. He changed the channel again. I brought up my dress slightly, parted my legs, and brought the purring device to caress my inner folds. The gentle vibration of the device sent soothing Barry-Manilow-like low frequencies onto my pussy and beyond.

I returned my full attention to the TV screen. My bald butler raised his eyebrows and readjusted the way he sat in his chair. He placed the remote down in front of him, then unzipped his pants. With his right hand, he pulled out his humongous black cock and started taming it, slowly. I felt an uncontrollable smile grow on my face.

Seems we're both playing the same one-player game.

The tip of my golden dildo fell into my pussy, tingling my opening as I pushed it in a little more. I looked down at myself, spreading open my lips as I watched the golden apparatus come out of me, wet from my own juices. I cranked the speed up a notch and prodded myself some more, trying to find just the right spot. I adjusted my hips on the seat. With a fling of my fingers, I undid the strap of my left sandal and brought my naked foot up onto the bench. My dildo had found just the spot. I cranked up the speed some more, both on the device and on my own prodding motions.

I stared at my bald man giving himself a beating. His own speed increasing as well... until he stopped. He let go off himself, then stared right at the camera and made a "come here" motion with his fingers before pointing at his erect cock.

Poor thing. He shouldn't leave that huge cock standing there, all alone!

Without thinking, I reached down to undo my other sandal then rushed to the reception area— bare feet and pussy dripping wet— before someone else could claim my large, erect prize.

THE TALL, bald butler got up from behind the desk as I approached.

"You were watching me, weren't you?"

"Maybe," I said between hurried breaths. My chest heaved as my breathing returned to normal. From where I stood, I couldn't tell if he'd hidden his cock or if it was still out in the open. I wanted that wooden reception desk to dissipate instantly so I could jump his bones already.

"No need to pretend," he said with a smile. "From here I can see what channel everyone's room is tuned on."

"Interesting," I said before biting my lips. I

looked down and realized I was still holding on to my purring vibrator.

"And...," he started before walking away from me along the counter. He pushed an access panel that allowed him to join me on my side of the counter. "I could see that you were enjoying that golden dick," he said while taking it away from my hand. He turned it off and stuck it upright on the counter next to us. "Would you like to trade it in for a black one?"

I looked at him. There it was. His bare, glorious shaft pointed upward at a 45-degree angle, out of his pants' zipper opening as he walked closer toward me. I swallowed hard to prevent my own saliva from dripping out of my mouth. It certainly wasn't golden, but its shape and foreskin made me appreciate that some men really do look like their cocks... Big, huge, and bald. But right now, I wanted his humongous shaft more than anything—as long as it didn't come with a whip and restraints.

He kept walking but stopped within a foot of me. He pushed my hair back behind my shoulders and looked down at me.

"Beautiful dress. Looks great on you," he said while sliding the back of his hand along my neck, then along the skin of my exposed chest. His hand kept gliding down. He lowered himself and rested his knees on the *Welcome* mat on which I had stood during check-in earlier today. His hand found its way to the slit of my dress while his other hand lifted up and bunched the fabric off to the side. He blew onto my pussy as he approached it, his warm breath feeling delicious among the cool air of the castle. His adept tongue traced my lips and tickled my clit, but it wasn't what I needed.

"Enough foreplay," I said between moans. "I need you inside of me now!"

He pulled his head away from my pussy and looked at me, his fiery eyes in agreement with my request. He dug in his pant pocket and retrieved a condom, which he quickly donned.

"Come down," he said, his hands on my hips, pulling me down toward him. He sat on the mat. I hiked up my dress and parted my legs so I could position myself around him. My knees on both sides of his hips, I lowered my pussy onto his huge shaft. I delighted when my insides parted, swallowing almost all of his length. I was so wet that even his huge girth slid into me like it belonged there. I rocked my hips toward the front for a second, wanting my clit to rub against him, then pulled myself up again. Slowly. Until he almost came out of me. Then, I slid down that pleasure pole, again and again. Each time faster. His hands dug my breasts out of my dress and I let them bounce away as my hungry pussy feasted on his large cock. Out of habit, one of my hands reached down to my clit. I had to flick it. I had to build up the pleasure. I had to come before him.

He moaned. He grunted. Then an orgasm enveloped my senses, forcing me to become still, save for the uncontrollable shivers. He took over the motions, thrusting his hips upward into me as my insides kept convulsing. He kept ravishing me as my entire insides pulsated in pleasure. My yelps of joy echoed in the large entrance hall, then his climax joined my chorus. I let myself fall on my side, the tiled floor cooling my quivering body. His hips had followed my fall, turning slightly. My hands went to my exposed breast. My ecstasy and pounding heart were making them heave out of control, but it was nothing compared to my throbbing pussy. I could feel it kneading convulsively onto the butler's cock, which it still held hostage.

"How I love my job!" said the butler, bursting my orgasmic bubble.

AFTER DOING UP MY DRESS, my pussy finally satisfied, I agreed to partake in the champagne the butler offered. How grateful was I for that enormous itch to have been scratched!

"Fancy seeing what people are up to? Or what they're watching?" he asked.

Curiosity had the best of me. "Sure," I said.

He sat on the chair behind the desk, then tapped on his lap to invite me to join him.

I did, wrapping an arm around his muscular shoulders.

He flipped through the channels of the small TV screen that had been installed on the desk below the computer monitor. With a click of a mouse followed by a swift flight of fingers across the keyboard, he made tabulated data appear on the monitor.

"See? I can see your room is still tuned to the reception area, but nobody's in your room now," he said after flicking to the video camera in my bedroom. I hadn't seen a camera in there, but based on the angle, it had to be located just above the fireplace.

"Looks like two rooms are watching the dungeon and another is watching the spa."

He grabbed the remote again, flipping through more channels.

"Stop," I said as I recognized Lucie and her husband. The two of them were sitting at the foot of their bed, a bucket of champagne next to them, with three flutes.

"Shoot! I was supposed to join them after dinner," I said.

"There's still time."

I got up, and he slapped my ass. My golden dildo stared at me from the desk. I hesitated for a second then grabbed it before rushing away.

"Mind if I watch?" his words echoed unanswered as I climbed up the stairs, feeling my juices dripping out of my slightly sore pussy.

11:20 P.M.

I WENT DOWN the main hallway, but continued past my bedroom until I saw number 6. I approached the door and brought up my hand to knock, but the first tap of my fist pushed the door open. The wooden door squeaked as I opened it some more.

"Lucie?" I asked.

"*Entre ma chère!*" she said, inviting me to come in.

I walked in and closed the door behind me. Their room was similar to ours, furnished with oversized, hand-carved, wooden pieces but decorated in shades of forest green instead of burgundy. As I'd seen on the security footage, Lucie and Jean-Michel were sitting in front of their bed. They'd tossed a dozen cushions on the carpet in front of the fireplace. He'd taken off his tuxedo jacket, bow tie, shoes, and socks. I looked around the room in search of clues to see if this couple was into pain or had objects similar to those I'd seen in the dungeon a.k.a. torture room. I let out a discreet sigh once I realized I couldn't see such items here.

Lucie, still wearing the same burgundy dress, got up and walked toward me, a large smile on her face. The room was obviously warmer here, her nipples hiding quietly underneath the fabric of her gown.

"Welcome, please come and join us," she said, taking my golden dildo out of my hand.

What I was about to do came with a ton of questions that piled up in my head faster than I could answer them.

How is this supposed to work? Should I approach her? Him? How does protection work here? Oooh... I should probably clean up first. Couldn't say that I'd had sex with different people so soon one after another before, but I knew I should definitely clean up. *Isn't this what bidets are for?*

I suddenly realized Lucie had addressed me in English, so I asked her why while she led me to the cushions in front of the fireplace, holding me by the hand.

"Because that's part of Jean-Michel's fantasy. He wants to have a threesome with a gorgeous foreigner."

I could feel my cheeks warm up. Guess I'd never learn to take a compliment without blushing.

Fingers grazing against my arm made me realize that Jean-Michel was now standing behind me.

"Very gorgeous foreigner..." He walked slowly around me, his touch a soft breeze on my skin. He approached my neck; I heard him inhale my scent. He brushed a hand through my hair, then brought it all to rest in front of me on one shoulder. His fingers traced my neck then slid down below my nape. His hand kept lowering until it reached the small of my back. He twirled me in front of him. After the slow revolution was over, his light brown eyes sparkled, his lips parted slightly, and he took in another deep breath, making me feel like a fine bottle of wine he was assessing for an award. He pulled me in closer, and his free hand traced the outline of the dress's fabric, caressing the exposed portion of my breasts.

His eyes were questioning me, but his mouth

remained quiet. His gaze went from my eyes, to my lips, to my cleavage, then back to my lips. He smelled like a temple in exotic Bali.

He approached, his mouth closer to mine. I could hear his heavy breathing, the warm air of his exhalations brushing against my skin.

I finally came out of my paralyzed state. "Listen, Jean-Michel," I said. "I think I should clean up first. You know..."

It took him a second to register my words, but then his eyebrows went up. "*Oui*, of course! Why don't you take a bath? I'm sure Lucie can pour one for you."

She grabbed me by the hand and led me into their bathroom. Instead of being peach-colored, theirs was light green, but the same attention had been given to the exquisite, luxurious decor.

"Let's pour you a bubble bath. Don't you think that would be nice?" Without waiting for my reply, she grabbed a few bottles from the vanity and return to the bathtub. She bent down to the center of the tub where the knobs and drain were located. She adjusted the water temperature, then plugged the tub and let the water run. Once about an inch of water filled the tub, she emptied the small bottle of light green liquid and it foamed instantly.

Lucie turned around and approached me. Her hands came up and framed my face.

"You're so pretty. A true, natural beauty," she said before letting go of me.

She then felt up the sides of my dress until she found the small zipper. With an expert hand, she undid it and released my breasts from my gown's corset-like restraints. I pushed down the dress past my hips and stepped out of it. Lucie picked it up and draped it over the back of the vanity chair as I stepped into the tub. The water was exquisite, but the expansive foam was already reaching the edges of the tub. I turned off the water. An aroma of freshly baked apples filled the air. I let my body sink into the water, which was not as deep as I'd expected it to be. The water barely reached my hips. The rest was all light, foamy, scented bubbles.

Lucie came back toward me, a large hair clip in hand. She expertly wrapped my hair and clipped it in a loose chignon to prevent it from getting wet. Then she undid her dress, her eyes locked onto mine as she disrobed. Her cute breasts were perkier than a teenager's. Her dark nipples came out to greet the cooler air of the bathroom. Like most of the European women I'd seen on various beaches, her upper body displayed no tan lines. With a flick

of her hips, she pushed down the stretchy dress and stepped out of it, leaving me a full frontal view of her narrow, blonde landing strip.

Just as she'd done with my dress, she bent down to take her gown then draped it on top of mine on the back of the chair.

She walked up to the tub and stepped into the opposite end. "Mind if I join you?" she asked after the fact.

I heard footsteps and turned around. Jean-Michel had walked in. He headed to the vanity and moved our dresses onto the small desk to clear the chair onto which he sat, facing us.

Lucie turned on the water once more and grabbed the flexible shower head and released it from its holder. She turned the brass fitting around the head and adjusted the water to a wide pattern, which she then sprayed on my chest, destroying some of my bubbly cover until she exposed my left breast. Then my right. She let go of the shower head, which fell somewhere among our limbs. Her hands reached up and cupped my breasts.

"I'd love to have breasts like those," she said as she gently kneaded them. She adjusted her position, going up on her knees, which both fit between my parted legs. She bent down toward me and licked some of the foam off of me. She backed up after a few licks, once again looking at me. The water level increased slowly, pushing more foam onto my chest and covering me once more. Lucie's hand dove underneath the surface and I felt one hand graze my pussy for a split second. Then she retrieved the shower head and adjusted the spray, this time to a pulsating jet.

"My favorite setting," she said, straightening up on her knees and bringing the jet toward her. The foam that had previously covered her groin disappeared instantly. She aimed the jet right at her pussy with one hand. With the other, she parted her thin pink folds. She was a miniature woman even in the smallest details. She closed her eyes, then took in a deep breath, her small breast moving, her nipples even perkier than before. She sighed as she exhaled, her mouth wide open.

"Don't be selfish now, Lucie," Jean-Michel ordered from his corner.

Lucie smiled and reopened her eyes. "Of course not." She redirected the shower head at me. The strong jet first hit my stomach, then she lowered it. The deeper it had to go into the depth of the water, the weaker the jet got. I reached my hand toward the drain. I pulled on the chain and waited, feeling the strength of the jet getting stronger as the water level dropped. The foam however, had remained attached to both of our bodies, except for where the jet was aimed.

I closed my eyes, enjoying the pulsating jet expertly being guided by Lucie. I felt her delicate fingers circling my outer lips, cleaning me up. Then, a demanding mouth suckled on my left breast. The roughness of the skin and the exotic smell told me it wasn't Lucie who was nibbling on my upper body. I reopened my eyes and saw Jean-Michel bent over the edge of the tub. His large hands tightened their grip around my breasts, squeezing them while Lucie had started probing my pussy with her digits.

The pulsating jet, the probing fingers, the nibbling of my nipples... It was all too much. With my body still blushed from my very recent orgasm, the experience overwhelmed my senses in a flash.

I screamed as I convulsed. "Oh myyyy goooddd!"

I pushed away the jet and Lucie's hand before cupping my pussy to protect my sensitive, engorged clit and lips. I moaned in pleasure as I tried to gain control of my breathing again. When I opened my eyes, Lucie's cute, tiny ass was stepping out of the tub. Jean-Michel backed away and got up. His cock tented his black pants as he bent his arms into what was left of the apple-scented foam. One arm under my knees and the other around my back, he lifted me out of the tub and brought my drained body over to the cushions in front of the fireplace.

He unbuttoned his shirt and tossed it aside. His pants and underwear soon followed suit. While Jean-Michel was getting naked, Lucie was busy picking up after him. She hung his clothes on a hanger. *I guess there are no rules to threesomes, OCD cleaning routines included.* I returned my attention to Jean-Michel who straddled me on my stomach, although his weight—thankfully—rested on his own legs. He cradled his cock between my breasts, then squirted sandalwood-scented oil all over my chest. The coolness of the oil surprised me, but his hands soon massaged my skin and warmed me back up. He then buried his cock deep in my cleavage before starting to drive himself back and forth between my breasts. He squeezed them together, tightening the gap and probably enhancing his experience. Among the slurping noises of his back-and-forth motions between my oil-covered breasts, I heard the gentle roar of my golden dildo getting closer. I glanced to my left and saw Lucie playing with the device as she knelt and approached me.

A few seconds later, I felt the familiar poke of the golden device fill my pussy. I brought my hand to Jean-Michel's bare chest, my fingers skimming the light layer of hair between his pecks as he kept tit-fucking me. He suddenly let go of me and slapped my left breast. Hard. "Whoa!" I yelped, watching it bounce from his slap.

"Sorry," he said before squeezing my breasts even tighter together and grinding himself into them faster. With each deep push, I saw his pink, glistening head poking toward my face. I stuck my tongue out and stretched it, as though I could tickle it if only I timed it right. Then, without notice, he gushed out onto my face and into my open mouth. He grunted and kneaded my breasts some more while I licked his salty, gooey treasure off of my face.

And just then, Lucie cranked up the speed on my golden device, while she suckled on my clit, bringing on yet another tidal orgasmic wave to wash over my body.

I HUGGED Matt prior to him boarding his flight, a light pinch stinging my chest.

Matt had been a great partner for several encounters, but it was probably time to call it quits. I was unsure if I could keep seeing him without feeling like I was preventing him from fully experiencing all of the things he truly enjoyed... Or perhaps I'd risk getting attached to his good looks and fall back to my past, needy behaviors.

I watched his firm ass walk away and join the file of passengers that trickled through the flight attendants' check. His tall body, his broad shoulders, his ocean-scented hair, his fantastic cock, his skilled tongue... I'd miss him, that was for sure.

I smiled and waved at him just as he looked my way after having his ID checked by the flight attendant.

I let out a sigh. That was that. *Goodbye, Matt.*

I turned around and flicked a piece of lint from my uniform.

Time to get ready for work. My own flight would depart in four hours.

As I walked away toward the shops and restaurants in search of a decent cup of coffee, I thought about what I'd seen and done this weekend. I'd made some progress with my sexual life (and definitely kept up with my higher self-esteem), but I also felt like I'd only seen the tip of the iceberg, like I was a virgin of sorts when it came to certain sexual acts.

There were so many new experiences I still had to try.

Multiple partners at once I think I could really enjoy, but S&M and bondage... Can't knock it until I try... But I'm definitely not ready for that yet.

A hot British Airways pilot smiled at me as we crossed paths. I'd never seen him before, but I felt my pussy twitch just thinking about the fun I could have with him in bed. It wasn't the first uniformed man who had me fantasizing at first glance.

Guess I have a weakness for airline captains?

I had to figure out a way to scratch that itch without making a reputation for myself. After all, captains were at the top of the hierarchy once in the air.

Is having sex with authority figures my fetish? Or is it the captain's uniform that turns me on? Or something else? I'm sure Freud would have something clever to say about it.

PART TWO

MY XXX EXPERIENCE

THE PLAN

MY STEWARDESS'S last entry puzzled me, especially her having a thing for airline captains. *Does she know me? Have our paths crossed before? Did she purposefully drop her diary in* my *bag?*

If only time travel existed... I could simply turn around and look at her face (and the rest of her...) But it's impossible, so it leaves me with the following options for now:

OPTION 1: Determine which airline employs my stewardess by reviewing their onboard duty-free offerings and eliminating those that don't offer a Dior perfume set.

First, that would be a lot of airlines to check (not to mention tedious work); and second, current airline offers may not be the same as last month's, last year's, or those of whenever she wrote that journal entry.

Likelihood of success: Close to nil.

OPTION 2: Deduce her employer by eliminating airlines that don't fly into Dublin/DUB and other airports she's flown to based on her journal entries.

Theoretically, that *could* help, but with shared flight codes and airline partners... It would still be useful to know if she was part of Star Alliance, SkyTeam, or Oneworld, though. The task of determining her exact airline (and her identity) would then be a little easier. But I can't do much with the information I have to date. And what if she's changed airlines for some reason?

Likelihood of success: Close to nil.

OPTION 3: Go to the one-of-a-kind castle in Ireland and track her down.

Jackpot! I know the name of this unusual castle. As to whether or not I'll be able to retrieve any useful information from the staff... Who knows? But definitely worth a try. Can't wait to ravish all of these hot maids. Is there a better way to retrieve information?

Likelihood of success: Average to high.

I can't wait to get to the Emerald Isle and start my all-inclusive fuck fest.

WHAT HAPPENED

I DID FIND that special Irish castle, but I've since redacted its name from her diary (should it ever fall into the wrong person's hands). Last thing I'd want is for this place to become popular with butt-ugly, lame-in-bed tourists. That would destroy one of the last few, true, remaining Wonders of the World.

I was planning to travel alone so I could take advantage of all the amenities on my own time, but when I called to book a room for a long weekend that coincided with one of my scheduled layovers, the receptionist informed me in her velvety Irish-accented voice that it was a very romantic hotel, so the castle only catered to couples. Hearing her words (and imagining the red-headed body that came with it) got me hard in seconds. Couldn't wait to get there.

But that meant that I had to find myself a woman to accompany me on the trip, a great-looking one if at all possible. Since I don't have a stand-by, go-to woman I haven't discarded after the initial go, I figured I'd wait to see what my crew had in store for me and then pick the best looking of the bunch, at least of those who were into the *Pilot-Stewardess Mentoring Program* as I liked to call it. I needed to be careful though. The lawyers who provided our mandatory annual harassment training had scared me enough that I now only approached the cute ones who smiled at me. Normally, the ones who brought me lunch were a good bet.

And if not, I'm sure I could hire a good-looking escort once I set foot in Ireland.

12:00 P.M.

IT SEEMED the universe had received my request loud and clear (or at least, my lucky star still shone bright from above.)

A couple of hours into our flight, after getting a call that my meal would be served shortly, a knock was heard on the cockpit door.

Bob, my co-pilot, pressed the toggle switch to open the door then got up, letting the lunch-holding stewardess in. "Enjoy your meal," he told me. "I'm gonna stretch and take a long bathroom break. I'll be back in about fifteen."

He squeezed passed the tall brunette in the tight space and addressed her, "Can you keep my lunch warm and bring it to me in half an hour?"

She nodded and I invited the brunette to sit down on Bob's seat. As per airline policy (to avoid hijacking and other security breaches), I was not allowed to be alone in the cockpit, and the door always had to be locked.

So, there we were: a hot brunette with me in a small, locked space. But I had to be careful with my words. After all, the voice recorder was always active.

We chit-chatted about nothing for a few minutes while I ate. Between bites, I asked her about her plans: if she was going to stay for a few days, or if she was heading back right away. She said she had the weekend off.

Perfect.

"Do you have an itinerary? A place to stay, things you want to see?" I asked.

Her mouth went up in a frown as she shook her head. "Nah, I like to wing it. I'd like to visit the Guinness Brewery. Maybe go to that bar that U2 owns..."

I finished my last bite then wiped my mouth with my napkin. "Are you staying somewhere special?"

"Haven't booked anything. But it's low-season. I'm sure I'll find a room." She smiled at me in a way that could mean something.

Just so I'd have the benefit of the doubt should someone listen to the in-flight recording, I crumbled the aluminum foil that previously covered my meal as I spoke again. "I have reservations at a unique castle. I'm sure they could accommodate the both of us." I tossed the aluminum mess I'd created into my empty glass.

Ball's in her court.

"Accommodate the both of us," she repeated, a smirk on her face. "If you're inviting me to your bed, I hope you're a more straight-forward lover than that," she said, standing up then letting her hands graze up my pants.

I pulled on her arms to force her to bend toward me, then planted my lips onto hers, one of my hands reaching to squeeze her breast through her shirt.

Solid C-cup.

Her tongue blazed into my mouth. Her hand grabbed the nape of my neck. Then, without a reason that I could tell, she pushed me away and backed off.

"That's more like it," she said before winking at me. "I'll see you at the car rental desk?"

And just like that, she unlocked the door and exited the cockpit, leaving me wanting more.

But now was not the time or place. My co-pilot was coming back in.

12:15 P.M.

"SHE'S ALRIGHT," Bob said, his hand pointing toward the cockpit door that the stewardess had just closed on her way out. He took back his seat and buckled up.

I nodded and gave him the thumbs up while I chewed on the last bite of my dessert.

"And she's a brunette. Hey, you think she could be *the* woman you're looking for?"

"What?" I asked him while glancing at the console to ensure gauges and displays all read as they should.

"Your gal from the diary. Or have you given up?"

I shook my head. "Can't give up. You think she

could be the one?" I paused to think it over, remembering her exact appearance. Hair color and breast size were correct. She was fairly tall. *Really curvy ass, though. Unsure about that. The girls in Mexico would have mentioned that detail, no?*

"Still don't know her name?" Bob asked, interrupting my reflection.

"Sometimes I call her Stefanie, or Samantha, or Suzy..."

Bob's eyebrows went up. "You found out her name starts with an S?"

"No." I shook my head, wondering how I'd come up with those. *Mental association with the word stewardess...?* "Could be Julia, Barbara... Her name's not important. It's her body I care about... and her—"

Bob chuckled. "Her name could be George..."

I flicked the back of my hand against his shoulder.

He lifted his chin. "Serious man! What if some guy played a prank on you?"

I looked at him squarely: his face was stern, his eyes steady.

"How much money are you going to waste looking for her?" he asked.

"Come on, Bob! A prank *that* elaborate? The

hand-writing's too pretty to be a man's. And the girls I spoke to in Mexico, the video I found in L.A. She exists."

"Well... I still think you're wasting your time. You're chasing a ghost."

AS PROMISED, the tall brunette met me at the car rental desk.

She arrived right after I'd finished reviewing and signing the rental agreement. I watched her stroll toward me, carry-on in tow. *Could she be* the *stewardess?* I didn't remember ever crossing paths with her before today's flight. But maybe an even more attractive woman had distracted me at the time. She was pretty. And obviously open to having a good time. I eyed her slender legs as she quickly bridged the gap that separated us. She hadn't changed out of her uniform yet and neither had I. *What's another three hours in my work clothes?* I couldn't wait to get to my special castle. I could undress her to find out if her tits matched those of the picture I'd seen in Mexico. *Or would she just tell me if I asked? Or would she lie and stretch the mystery as far as she could?*

Keys in hand, I headed toward the car I'd been assigned. She followed.

"This is the one," I said, pointing at the silver Corolla a few feet in front of us. "What's your name by the way?" I asked her, turning around to look at her.

"Crystal," she said, flashing me her pearly whites.

Memories of a very special Crystal sliding around a brass pole in Florida flashed in my mind. *A name with potential.* I unlocked the car doors and popped the trunk with the keychain remote.

"It was my grandmother's name," she continued while pushing her bag's handle to retract it into its slot. "She died just before I was born, so my mom insisted on naming me after her."

So much for the mental image of my pole-dancing Crystal. It'd irreversibly been replaced by a gray-haired lady dusting her crystalware.

"And you?" she asked while I placed her bag in the trunk next to mine.

"I'm Charlie," I said with a smile. "Nice to officially meet you."

I took off my hat and jacket, which I then lay on top of our small suitcases in the trunk before closing it.

Once in the driver's seat, I oriented myself with the somewhat awkward positioning of the control, while she chitchatted some more about her grandma. I turned on the GPS and entered the castle's coordinates while her verbal deluge of useless information continued.

I started the engine, which granted me her silence, followed by a strange outburst of teenage-like excitement that came complete with clapping and bouncing up and down.

"Can't believe we're going to a castle!"

"Never been to one?" I asked, happy that the topic had moved away from her family.

"No, I've never been anywhere else in Ireland outside of Dublin."

Strike One. Or is she just lying?

We managed to stay on a semi-interesting topic for a while, but about twenty minutes later, she reverted back to her family.

"It's funny, my new brother-in-law, the one who now owns the farm I grew up on, was asking me——"

"At junction 9, use the left three lanes to take the N7 exit to Limerick/Cork/Waterford/N8/N9," said my GPS. I ignored what Crystal said next, focusing my attention on the unfamiliar road signs and ensuring I kept focused on reversing everything I knew about lane directions and driving behavior.

Amid the flat, suburban scenery that started filling my view on both sides of the motorway, I overheard bits and pieces of my guest's never-ending verbal diarrhea. If only I could plug that mouth with a piece of myself and shut her up. Hard to do while driving... *Should I ask her to blow me right this minute?*

"Do you keep a journal?" I asked her, opting for a different tactic and abruptly interrupting the tale of her second cousin's wedding.

She paused for a few seconds, so I turned to look at her. Confusion—or was it resentment?—lurched from her eyes. I returned my attention to the road.

"You mean like a blog?" she asked.

I shook my head. "No. Journaling. Writing stuff down on paper. Do you keep a personal diary?"

She scuffed. "Hell no! Who has time for that?"

If you were to shut up once in a while, hours would magically appear.

Strike Two. Well there goes that theory. She's not my stewardess... and actually, I'm relieved she isn't.

"So... other than family farms and weddings, what are you into?" I asked.

A solid two hours of celebrity gossip and fashion tips followed, save for the much-appreciated interruptions provided by my GPS. Its computerized voice was a delight to my ears. I couldn't care less about whatever that Kardashian woman that Crystal kept talking about had done or was doing unless she was sitting on my face—and doing so in total silence.

The following goes without saying: I was relieved beyond belief when we finally arrived at our destination.

"Wow! You weren't kidding. It's a real castle!"

She clapped again. *Argh.* Then she undid her seat belt and opened the door. I appraised her ass as she got out of the car. On a scale of 1 to 10, she deserved a solid 8 for hotness but got a -6 penalty for not knowing when to shut up or act like a grown woman.

I can ditch her soon enough, though. I'm sure the staff here will keep me entertained.

5:55 P.M.

A TALL BLOND butler opened the door for us and led us into the expansive entrance hall, which matched to a T what the stewardess had described in her journal. *So this place does exist...* A part of me had remained skeptical, but I'm an optimist and was hoping for the best.

Unfortunately, the butler didn't look anything like Liam Hemsworth. He obviously wasn't a tall, bald, black man either. But based on my guest's googly eyes, he was attractive.

I scanned the vast space, hoping to find someone I could recognize from the stewardess's diary. The woman behind the reception desk wasn't the red-headed woman I'd fantasized about. *Too bad.* But the strawberry-blonde little thing standing there was very hot nonetheless. *Her luscious bubble-gum colored lips would look stunning around my cock, her doe eyes looking up at me...* Her French-maid outfit was even better than the one I'd been picturing in my mind. With so little fabric, nip-slips had to be common workplace hazards.

While I admired the receptionist, my guest once again clapped like a stupid thirteen-year-old. I turned to look at her. She was twirling, her arms stretched out to her sides, her head tilted back to look up at the ceiling.

"Helloooo!" she called out, listening to her own voice bouncing and echoing against the stone walls.

Seriously?

I let her be and proceeded to greet the hot receptionist and check ourselves in.

6:00 P.M.

ONCE AGAIN, my hopes that Kate and/or Chloe would be the ones to bring up our bags got dashed.

Is my good luck gone?

The maids who'd been assigned to us were definitely hot and fuckable, though: Victoria was tall and skinny, her hair pitch black; Sharla was shorter, very curvy, and slightly oversized. *They wouldn't know my stewardess or be able to help me track her down. Guess I'll just have to get on with the program and make the most of my stay.*

We left our luggage with Victoria and were led up the stairs by the shapely Sharla.

Crystal's childish excitement kept growing the deeper we got in the entrance of the castle. She oohed and aahed at the tapestries hung by the staircase while going up. I admired the bare crotch above my head instead. She giggled like a young girl when she saw the large oil paintings lining the upstairs hallway. I mentally prepared myself for the tipping routine instead. *Will I get Victoria or Sharla?* Sharla's pussy sure looked inviting a few seconds ago.

Victoria arrived just on time with the luggage trolley. She met us in our room, then offered to unpack our bags.

I declined, but Crystal took her up on her offer. "And could you also pour me a bath, please?" she asked the tall and skinny maid.

"Of course, I'll run the bath," said Victoria, leaving our bags on the brass trolley. I watched the rounder maid grab Crystal's suitcase and place it on the bench at the end of the bed. I felt a little ungentlemanly to not offer to lift the carry-on bag, but, having taken it out of the trunk a few minutes earlier, I knew it was light, and I wanted to watch her bend down and contort her body in the tiny outfit. She proceeded with a smile, first unzipping the navy blue suitcase, then carefully unfolding the neatly folded shirts, skirts, and black underwear my guest had brought. Sharla then walked to the wardrobe to open it and retrieve a few hangers, stretched up to reach the pole, and then down, and... *Ding, ding ding! First nip-slip!* And a big one at that! By the time she had finished hanging all of Crystal's clothes, the maid's entire beautiful left tit hung loose.

"Um..." Chrystal said before clearing her throat.

"Anything else I can help you with?" Sharla asked Crystal.

Crystal's hand flew up in the air, rotating around her own breast. "You're... You're... showing," she finally said.

The rounder maid looked down at her breasts, then her eyebrows went up. "It'd probably be better if I evened things out, don't you think?" she said before pulling out her other round tit from her dress.

"That's not what I meant!" Crystal said, her eyes going from Sharla to me, then back to Sharla who was walking toward Crystal while massaging her swollen, natural globes.

"You don't like them?" Sharla asked. "Why don't you show me yours so your captain friend here can tell us if our bodies are beautiful."

Crystal was now more confused than ever.

"I want to play, too!" said Victoria as she came back in the room. I turned toward her as she pulled down her top, exposing her small, perky breasts.

"What kind of place is this?" Crystal asked, her face red, her voice approaching the boiling point.

"First time I guess." Victoria frowned, then covered her small boobs. She walked over to one of the nightstands and retrieved a black leather binder, which she handed to Crystal.

Sharla's hand placed most of her left tit back in her dress, and she was about to cover her other large, pink nipple. "No!" I said, taking a few steps toward her so I could caress her fleshy mountains of natural goodness before it was too late.

"Ah, I see the captain may be interested in our services." Sharla smiled at me, her hand pulling down her dress and re-exposing her beautiful mounds. I kneaded them and pinched her nipples.

From the corner of my eye, I saw Crystal march into the bathroom, binder in hand. The door slammed shut behind her. I couldn't see where Victoria had gone to, but it didn't matter. Those gorgeous DDD-cups were out of this world. I was about to bend down to suckle on them when Sharla pulled on my tie and backed up toward the bed, taking me along with her. She landed on her back. I landed on top of her, on the world's most comfortable pair of cushions. My erect shaft pushed against the fabric of my pants, but Victoria suddenly reappeared, her hand reaching between me and Sharla, undoing my belt, then pulling down my zipper.

I lifted myself off from the beautiful tits and brought up the bottom of her crinoline dress. There it was, the pussy I'd seen while climbing the stairs, in all of its bare glory. I heard a drawer sliding nearby. I turned and saw Victoria reach into the nightstand and retrieve a handful of condoms, which she placed next to Sharla on the bed. Victoria then climbed onto the bed. She placed a pillow underneath Sharla's head, then knelt herself squarely above Sharla's face before lifting her dress up in the front and exposing herself to me. Her black stockings were held up by black garters. Her matching black bush had been trimmed into a small V, or perhaps an arrow pointing down. Sharla was looking up, her fingers grazing Victoria's pussy while another hand was groping her own exposed breasts. Sharla's bald pussy was spread open for me to inspect or do as I wish with.

Best Irish scenery ever.

The bed was at the perfect height for me. I

suited up my cock with one of the condoms, then gently pulled Sharla's pussy closer to the edge of the bed. Victoria took care of repositioning the pillow, then herself while the tip of my cock made a recon move into Sharla. I probed her gently and slowly at first, taking in the view and pacing myself. I let my hands seize her humongous tits while my hips began their regular thrusting rhythm. Her tunnel was tight, slippery, and wet. I brought my hands back to her legs and pussy, parting her thighs some more, bringing one of her legs to rest on my shoulder, then parting her folds. I licked my fingers before bringing them to her clit. I teased it while looking at my cock sliding in and out of her. Sharla started moaning. I increased my cadence. I started pounding her harder and harder, watching her huge boobs bounce out of control while she sloppily ate her counterpart's pussy.

In between slurping and sucking noises, whenever Sharla came up for air, juices glistened on her cheeks and chin. Above her face, Victoria started squealing like an ambulance siren. One hand rubbed at her own clit while she twisted one of her nipples. I throttled Sharla's clit with my thumb while ramming her. I felt Sharla's pussy clench around my cock. Her head pulled away from

Victoria's pussy. Her back arched, bringing her tits up, even though they still spilled over to her sides. She squeezed them together as she came in a loud scream. That was all I could take. I gave her my all and came into her pulsating pussy.

While my heartbeat returned to normal, my senses came back to reality. Sharla's mouth had returned to her friend's pussy. Victoria's squeals had reached new levels. She closed her eyes and her cries stopped suddenly. I watched her face contort in silence as her hips quivered above Sharla's head.

I wonder if turndown service will be the same?

AFTER THE MAIDS reminded me of the upcoming dinner that started at 7 p.m. sharp, they left me—fully satisfied.

I did up my pants and decided to check on Crystal.

I walked over to the bathroom door and gently rapped on it. "Crystal, can I come in?" I asked.

A few seconds elapsed, making me wonder if she'd left the room unnoticed while I was doing the maids.

"Yes," she said, finally.

I pushed open the door and saw her coming out of the tub, butt naked, a few clouds of foam still attached to her firm, young, and beautiful body. For a few seconds, I admired her curves, her tan, her tits, and her pussy. She actually deserved higher than an 8, especially now that her mouth was closed. Her tits, although beautiful, confirmed that she wasn't my stewardess.

"Like what you see?" she asked while reaching toward a large white towel than hung nearby. Her C-cups had yet to display the damages of gravity.

I smiled at her. "Indeed."

She wrapped her body into the towel, forcing me to look away from it and notice her stern face. Her stare was icy. Her lips flat.

"You're mad?" I asked.

Her hands flew up as she shook her head, her eyes now perfect circles, her mouth agape. "You brought me to a whore house and you don't expect me to be mad?"

"Last I checked, I'm the one paying the bill. You accepted my invitation, and you seemed eager to get to know me better..."

She snorted. "I was looking forward to having sex with *you*, Charlie. Not the maids!"

"Well... this place is an open-bar," I said. "Me, maids, butlers, other guests... You can have whoever your cute little pussy fancies."

"So I read," she said, her head pointing at the binder sitting on the vanity.

Her comment had me curious. I headed toward the vanity and picked up the leather binder. The cover was soft. On it were engraved, in gold letters, the words *Rules of Conduct*.

I flicked past the first few pages, then stopped on a numbered list:

1- Have the decency to protect yourself and our staff. A large supply of condoms is provided free of charge in all rooms.

2- If someone doesn't want you, be respectful and walk away.

3- Open your mind. Try new things and new people.

4- We will not be held liable for unwanted pregnancies or medical claims.

5- For emergencies that are not related to your being horny, dial 1-1-2.

I put the binder down, not wanting to read anything that would remove the mystique from what I was so eager to experience.

"By the way, dinner starts in..." I paused to look

at my watch, "...twenty minutes. There are evening gowns in the wardrobe. Formalwear is required."

She grunted as she stepped out of the bathroom.

I took it as a sign that she had registered the information, then undressed and stepped in the shower.

I needed to freshen up for dinner.

DRESSED IN A TUXEDO, and with a slightly angry but thankfully-still mute guest on my arm, I headed down to the great hall.

Classical music aired in the room that bore its name extremely well: it *was* great. Twenty or so people—all dressed in penguin suits or sexy gowns—were mingling, champagne flutes in hands.

I grabbed two glasses at the first opportunity, temporarily stepping away from my guest to do so. When I backtracked to offer her a drink, she was gone. A quick scan of the room told me she was headed toward a blond, muscular man whose neck was as wide as his square face. He was sitting on the arm of a large leather chair, chatting with another champagne-holding man.

Good riddance.

Now... What lovely lady will have the pleasure of getting to know me better tonight? The options were numerous, but I had to pick an open-minded woman. *I don't want another Crystal.* A wild-haired brunette reached me before I had made a decision.

"Are you going to drink them both?" she asked, her head pointing at my extra champagne flute. Below the tangled mess of her curls, the twinkle in her mascaraed eyes and her thick bright lips screamed *good time.*

"This one's for you," I said, handing her a glass. "I'm Charlie, by the way."

"Heather. Nice to meet you." She picked up the flute I was offering then clinked it against mine. A sip later, she licked her lips. "First-time?"

I nodded. "You?"

"I'm a convert. I come here every three months or so."

I eyed her up and down. Her ivory skin hadn't seen much sun. She wore a navy blue dress that consisted of two small bunches of fabric going from her shoulders to her hips, where they merged and widened to continue as the bottom of her dress. I couldn't see her legs at all, the flowing fabric reached the floor, but those two small bunches of fabric left an expansive V-neck that sank all the way down to her pierced navel. The fabric barely covered the center of her breasts, leaving the curvatures of her natural, perky, drop-shaped tits hanging visibly on both sides.

Although the only thing I wanted was to dig those breasts out, I restrained myself. After all, I had to act the part: I was wearing a tux. "Any tips for a first-timer?"

"Go with the flow. And... Actually, during the meal, if anything happens, just close your eyes and enjoy. You won't believe how heightened your other senses are when you—"

"Ladies and gents," said a deep voice a few feet away from me. I turned and saw a red-headed butler. "Please have a seat. We will begin with the first course shortly."

"Shall we?" I asked my new friend Heather, sliding my arm between her arm and body, grazing her soft white skin in the process.

I led her to the table and helped her with her seat, taking the opportunity to get an aerial view of her cleavage as I pushed her chair forward. Her stomach was totally flat, her piercing twinkled in the distance past her breasts. I inhaled to take in her scent: fresh-cut flowers.

I then sat myself on my guest's left. A man had taken the seat to my left.

A few seconds later, a dozen French maids came into the room, steaming bowls in hand. A petite blonde with huge breasts that reminded me of Pamela Anderson's brought my bowl with a large smile, and, as I looked at Heather's maid, I realized she too was being served by a petite, big-breasted, blonde maid. *Twins? That can't be!*

"New staff, again!" I heard Heather say.

I brought my attention back to the crazy-haired brunette. "High personnel turn-over?" I asked her.

"Seems like it. Unsure if unwanted pregnancies could be to blame," she said.

"Since you like this place so much, have you ever considered... working here?" I asked, making small talk, but mostly trying to gauge if she'd want to join me later for some after-dinner treats.

She pursed her lips, her eyebrows went up. She looked excited about the idea.

"There are certain... perks that are only available here, so it would be nice. But clients would keep me busy most of the time, so I wouldn't be able to enjoy what I like as often as I want."

Intriguing. "Does this particular perk have a name?" I asked.

I swear, her skin changed color as though the temperature had risen fifty degrees all at once. She fanned her hand in front of her. "Dustin," she finally said.

I looked around the room. There had to be a dozen menservants. I lowered my voice and asked, "Is he here right now?"

Her eyes widened. "In this room? God no!"

Her breasts were now heaving rapidly. Her hand moved faster to cool herself off, making the fabric of her dress sway... but not enough for my taste. *What is so special about this guy? How can he have that effect on a woman?*

I needed to know, if only so I could replicate his results. I kept probing. "So he's here at the castle but not in this room?"

As though a shiver had gone down her spine, her entire body shuddered. She inhaled deeply, once again forcing me to stare at her breasts as they rose. "I hope he still is." She dipped her spoon in her bowl, putting an end to my questions. At least for now.

A minute or so later, I finished my cream of vegetables and the same blonde waitress (or her twin sister?) picked up my empty bowl, brushing her large breast against my arm while she did.

Heather's obviously planning to hook up with that Dustin after dinner. Might as well work on my Plan B.

About a minute later, the tiny blonde waitress (or her twin) came back with a small plate of antipasto. This time, I allowed myself to grab a feel. Very firm, too firm to be natural, but I wasn't a judgmental guy. She winked at me when our eyes met.

Gotta love this kind of service.

A few plates later, the most anticipated course finally arrived.

I saw Heather's body jerk first, then she said, "Remember to close your eyes."

I did.

I felt my legs slowly being parted, then a body squeezed between them. The sound of my zipper getting undone seemed louder than it should have been. I instinctively coughed to cover it up. An expert hand quickly brought me up to speed. Then, the warmth of a hungry mouth swallowed my cock. A tongue flickered. A hand held the base of my shaft as the open mouth feasted on me. *Is it one of the blonde twins?* Skillful fingers circled and clamped my balls with the exact pressure I needed. The lips and tongue kept at it, their warm embrace sometimes spiraling around me, sometimes deep-throating me. I had kept my hands on the table in front of me until now, but could no longer resist. The stimulation—or perhaps my heightened senses—had grown my excitement much faster than it normally did. I was about to come. I wanted to grab the woman's head and hold on to her hair. *Best head I've ever received in my life.* I let go of the table and reached for the head in my crotch just as I came, squirting my juices into the mouth of my...

I froze when I felt the short hair. I opened my eyes and saw large rectangular hands—one of which was still wrapped around my cock. A young, brown-haired, baby-faced man pulled away from me. Some of my come must have overflowed out of his mouth. It was dripping off of his chin. He smiled at me before disappearing under the table cloth and away from my legs.

What the fuck?

Heather's exalted cries made me turn to look at her. I swallowed hard. She had parted the front of her dress, her back was arched, and her hands were cupping her beautiful, now fully exposed breasts. Her small nipples pointed to the sky. That sight should have delighted me, hell it should have made me want to stand up and grab them. Eat them. But I couldn't move right now. I blinked. Repeatedly. My heartbeat was still racing. Was it just from my orgasm? *What the heck has just happened?* I looked to the man sitting on my left. He was still busy, couldn't care less about what had just happened to me. The head that bobbed on his lap had long brown hair. *Lucky.* I kept swallowing harder and harder, as though it would make me feel better. But it didn't.

Was it the certainty of my heterosexuality I could no longer swallow?

I MISSED most of what happened during the fifteen minutes that followed. If any of the kinky stuff that my stewardess had described occurred, I totally missed it, dealing with accepting the fact that I'd just had my first male-to-male encounter... and it had felt good? Better than good, actually... I pushed those thoughts down past my brain's non-return valve.

I came back to my senses as the butler was reaching Heather's seat, hat in hand.

"Is Dustin available?" she asked him.

"Yes, he is. Ready as usual in the stable."

In the stable? Was Dustin a farmhand?

"Good. He'll be my dessert, then." Heather's

chest once again started heaving profusely. This time, she brought one of her hands into her dress, squeezing her breast. She closed her eyes. I could hear her heavy breathing from my seat.

What the heck is so special about this guy?

The butler walked toward me and offered his hat. I was glad he was red-headed and therefore not the guy who'd given me the best blow job I'd ever had. I retrieved my dessert:

Spa treatment: Pick one (or more) of the staff and enjoy an all-inclusive spa treatment of your choice.

A few minutes later, people started pulling away from the table. I stood up and headed toward the first twin I found to make sure nobody else was going to claim her.

I handed her my paper slip. "Would you and your sister be interested in joining me at the spa?" I asked.

She smiled at me, exposing her white teeth for the first time this evening. "We'd love to. We've been chatting about you all evening. Meet us down by the pool in about twenty minutes?"

She gave me instructions on how to find the

pool, then I looked at my watch. I had some time to kill.

Why not find out what was so special about that Dustin? I'd love for women to get flustered like that just by thinking about me.

I LEFT the great hall via a door that led to the courtyard.

Once outside, I noticed a faint smell of manure indicating that farm animals did live near the castle. I looked around and saw the silhouettes of a few buildings against the falling dusk. A horse neighed in the distance. The noise had to have come from the stable, so I headed in that direction.

The closer I got, the louder and more frequent the neighs occurred. Then, Heather's moans joined suit. When she screamed to god a split second before the horse neighed and hoofed again, I froze.

Shit. I suddenly understood who Dustin was.

I turned around and hurried back toward the

castle as though the farther I got from the stable, the faster the unthinkable mental image I was seeing would disappear.

I don't know for sure. I didn't see anything. But wouldn't it rip her open? Is it even feasible?

I shook my head. For all I knew, she could have been playing with herself while looking at its cock. Or maybe there was a farmhand called Dustin and a horse just happened to be neighing while the two people were going at it.

Yeah. Let's just leave it at that. I didn't want to think about this a second more.

I WAS BEGINNING to regret coming to this castle, but once I got to the pool and saw my blonde twins wearing tiny red bikinis, I changed my mind.

Their four ballooned-breasts were near perfect spheres, with puny nipples poking through the undersized fabric. They were sitting on the side of the hot-tub, their legs dangling into the water. Their arms extended behind their backs, holding their torsos up, their breasts out. They were smiling at me.

I greeted them while trying to spot a trait that I could use to differentiate them, but I couldn't find anything. Both had soft green eyes, their long blonde hair was exactly the same length. The one's lips were just as luscious as the other's. Their tits were equally humongous and fake.

"I'm Deidre," said the one on the left.

"And I'm Cassandra," said the other.

"I'm Charlie," I said, taking off my jacket, then bow tie. "I don't want to be rude, but how can I tell who's who. You are both beautiful and... identical?"

"There's a very easy way," Cassandra said while pulling on the string of her sister's bottom. Deidre pulled on the other, then pushed down the fabric before spreading her legs open. "Deidre's got a bush," said Cassandra before pulling on both of her strings and sliding down her own bottom. "I don't."

"That will work. But seems like I've got some catching up to do," I said, hurrying my pace as I took off the rest of my clothes.

"Good! Join us when you're ready." Cassandra said before letting her body sink into the steamy tub.

Deidre slipped in beside her, then fully immersed herself in the water before coming back out. She then slicked her wet hair back, her back arched.

I looked away from them for a second, then smiled as I read a safety notice next to me advising patrons that birthday suits were not only allowed, but recommended.

When I turned to look at them again, the twins' beautiful faces were just out of the water. They were floating on their backs. What drew my attention were the floatation devices on their chest. Although still covered by their tops, the red fabric had shifted slightly, partly exposing a couple of their burnt-pink areolae. Their implants were just incredible. They could possibly save a drowning man's life. And with that view, I stepped into the tub, my cock at the ready.

I was glad to feel the warm water on my skin, but couldn't wait to feel their skin against mine. Their mouths, their gorgeous floatation devices, their warm pussies... Their *female* parts. Maybe the past two hours had somehow emasculated me... but I was determined to once again prove my heterosexual identity.

I stepped down once, then twice. After the third step, my dangling balls felt the warmth of the water, my cock seemingly floating toward them. I went further toward the center of the oversized tub—it was really more of a small pool with jets—reaching a deeper level.

The twins straightened up and circled me,

bouncing up and down slightly as they stepped around me. One after the other, I undid the knots that kept their farces-of-a-top on. I tossed the wet fabric onto the edge, then stuffed my face into Deirdre's chest. I could feel Cassandra's boobs pressed against my back while she wrapped her arms around my waist. She started feathering my cock with her fingers.

I came out of Deirdre's cleavage, then climbed up a couple of steps and lifted her out of the water to bring her ass onto the edge. She sat upright and I parted her legs and looked at her overgrown blonde pussy as it dripped. Cassandra moved to follow me. The light strokes of her fingers had morphed into a full fist around my shaft. I bent forward, bringing my mouth to Deidre's hairy pussy. Blowing on it while one of my hands irrepressibly went for one of her knockers. My tongue twitched there for a second, right at the opening of the wild jungle, ready to part its thick bush and clear the trail to Come Town.

"But what about me?" Cassandra whined behind me.

"Come out with me," I told her. Like a gentleman, I let her go first and watched her ass as she climbed out of the tub. As part of an uncontrollable reflex, my hand slapped her ass. She giggled.

I spotted towels rolled up on a side table and grabbed a few, which I unfolded and laid flat by the side of the tub. Condoms had also been thoughtfully placed here. After suiting up my cock, I took Cassandra by the hips and brought her onto the towel with me. I lay down on my back, holding her by the hand and then guiding her to sit on my erect shaft. She slowly made her way onto my pole in a squatting position. One move after another, she found her rhythm, sliding up and down my shaft like I was a carnival ride. I motioned to Deirdre to join us. She knelt down next to me, then stepped one knee over my face before lowering her Amazonian blonde jungle onto my hungry mouth.

I could no longer see their humongous boobs, but that was alright. I closed my eyes again, letting my other senses intensify the experience. Deirdre's juices salted my mouth while her musky scent inebriated me. I suckled on her. I flicked my tongue against her. I managed to squeeze up one of my arms from between her legs and bring it up to her pussy, parting her folds and then teasing her clit with my fingers. Her sister was still riding my shaft, but was no longer doing it in silence. Slowly but surely both sisters started moaning and groaning. Their quiet groans turned into pre-orgasmic sighs, gaining both in pitch and volume. Cassandra changed position. I felt cool air around my naked cock for a few seconds, then it was once again swallowed by her pussy. But she'd definitely changed my penetration angle. Her breasts brushed against my legs as she rode me downward in a potentially dangerous slant. But she rode me to the finish line with flying colors a minute after her sister came into my mouth.

Isn't it nice when sisters share everything?

THANKFULLY, I didn't have to deal with Crystal much more over the rest of our stay at the castle. She spent both of her nights in some other bedroom. She even managed to hitch a ride back to the airport with that muscular guy, which made me the happiest guy on earth (especially after a few more successful encounters with the female staff).

I was all packed up now, relaxing a little before checking myself out of this amazing castle.

As I looked out of the bedroom window, putting my thoughts down on paper to keep a record of my Irish experience, I let my gaze settle on a nearby church. The rising sun was shining its pink light just right to emphasize the church's large Celtic cross. In an odd way, the cross's shape represented the perfect woman for me: the intersection of intelligence with sex-appeal, combined with a little circle of craziness. Crystal was lacking in the first; Heather was overly gifted in the third. My stewardess appeared to have just the right balance for me. I'm certainly glad her journal didn't include any mention of Dustin. I'm well hung, but two-legged men can't compete with *that*.

I didn't learn anything new about my stewardess, which sucked.

But I'm glad to know she's obviously not the jealous kind like Crystal. A woman willing to share her man with other women had some sort of je-ne-sais-quoi.

Was it just me, or was it every man's fantasy? Such women seemed to be very few and far between... Of course, the castle's employees appeared to all share that rare quality.

But that stewardess... I couldn't wait to find her. I needed to put my obsession to rest. Maybe I'd get to know her a little first. Or not... But I definitely couldn't wait to thrust my cock in her warm pussy...

And this could happen very soon if I keep at it... If I keep following the clues from her diary.

NEXT STEPS

I RE-READ her next journal entry, and I'm still impressed by her ability to push her own boundaries and explore hidden territories.

It's hard to believe what the innocent woman who went camping with her boyfriend has turned into... Her layover in Thailand proves that she's certainly changed a lot since that camping trip. Her Thai spa experience is definitely... unique. At least I can't say that I've experienced that kind of massage in the past (in Thailand or in any other country). And, to be honest, I'm not sure if I'd want to experience *all* of it.

But I still have some data processing to do with respect to my own experiences. I'll deal with it some other time. I've gone beyond a line I didn't believe I'd ever cross. I don't think there's any possibility of going back after this... But for now, this fact is filed away, labeled as uncomfortable and raw data, into a different part of my brain.

My mystery stewardess has left me a few decent clues that should hopefully help me learn more about her identity. I think I'm getting closer to my goal: figuring out who she is so I can fuck her until my obsession disappears for good.

Better stock up on antacid as I'm planning on having quite a few spicy Thai meals in the near future.

TO BE CONTINUED...

...IN PART 6 of *The Stewardess's Diary*, available at most major book retailers.

The complete episodic novel is also available in one (thick) paperback with exclusive author's notes about the series and what inspired each episode.

ABOUT THE AUTHOR

S.M. Pratt is a single woman traveling the world on her own, living in the moment, looking for more than love, and always trying out new things. Fun adventures and unique cultural experiences are always at the top of her agenda, no matter the country she happens to be visiting.

She would love to quit her day job and write full-time. You can help her write the next story faster by purchasing her books and/or giving her five-star reviews. Without your support, she's invisible and unable to make a living doing what she loves, which is creating what you love to read.

If you haven't done so already, please join her private reader group for previews, exclusive offers, and more. It's free: https://smpratt.com

For more information:
smpratt.com
info@smpratt.com